BREAKER

BY
LOGAN CHANCE

Denise

— Enjoy —

Logan Chance

Copyright © 2017 by Logan Chance

All rights reserved. No part of this publication may be reproduced, distributed, or transmitted in any form or by any means, including photocopying, recording, or other electronic or mechanical methods, without the prior written permission of the publisher, except in the case of brief quotations embodied in critical reviews and certain other noncommercial uses permitted by copyright law.

Dedication

To anyone who has ever felt lost. May you find your way back home.

Table of Contents

Chapter One
Chapter Two
Chapter Three
Chapter Four
Chapter Five
Chapter Six
Chapter Seven
Chapter Eight
Chapter Nine
Chapter Ten
Chapter Eleven
Chapter Twelve
Chapter Thirteen
Chapter Fourteen
Chapter Fifteen
Chapter Sixteen
Chapter Seventeen
Chapter Eighteen
Chapter Nineteen
Chapter Twenty
Chapter Twenty-one
Chapter Twenty-two
Chapter Twenty-three
Chapter Twenty-four
Chapter Twenty-five
Chapter Twenty-six
Epilogue
Sneak Peek, Love Doctor
Acknowledgements

Chapter One

Booker

Of all the places I've been, this is the last place I want to be. But, here I am. Back at my childhood home. Back to sell this place. To move on and forget it.

It feels as though a million years have passed since I was last here. And maybe in some weird way it has. A million years worth of memories are suppressed neatly in the dark hollows of my mind.

A tall overgrowth of grass brushes across the lawn, the blades nicking my calves. As I trudge through, I can't keep my eyes off the paint-peeled, red door. Majestic and unyielding, larger than any other in this quiet neighborhood, it keeps the world out and its secrets tucked safely inside.

Thump. Thump. My heart pounds.

Welcome back the lock creaks out when I turn the key. Stale air suffocates me when I step inside. The large space seems coffin sized.

"This place is a dump," I mumble into the stillness.

The house has barely been touched since I left it as a kid.

First order of business, getting the power on. No way will I spend my time fixing up this hell hole without electricity.

As soon as I push the faded curtains aside in the main room, I see it, the ticket seller to this forgotten home—the Pacific Ocean with its dark blue water crashing over sleek, black rocks in the distance.

Life pumps and breathes outside this paned glass.

This view will be the reason buyers flock, hopefully offering more than my asking price.

Anxiety leaves an icy sheen of sweat on my forehead as I walk through the cavernous rooms, assessing. Floors groan under my footsteps. Dust skitters in the air. The marks notched in the doorframe of my old room wink at me as I pass.

Before I head out to the hardware store, I take inventory of the things I'll need: paint, drywall, tile, grout, a bed to sleep in. A handle of bourbon. It's going to be one hell of a fixup.

Lucky for me, I have all the time in the world.

The now outdated kitchen, once the artery of this house, needs the most work. I push the back slider open and step out onto the drab patio. The backyard isn't much to look at, a nine by nine concrete slab surrounded by encroaching weeds. This area needs to be the focal point at showings. People like the illusion of happy—pretty flowers and landscaping. Maybe I'll hire a gardener. Maybe even plant a bush here or there myself.

The wind tugs at my cargo shorts and black shirt, and I wander to the edge of the property.

Like it always does, the ocean beckons.

The Pacific wants a word with me. I oblige, following the dirt trail down to the shore. The problems with the house can wait. I need some alone time. Just me and my thoughts.

Not even bothering to remove my shoes, I step onto the sand. The sun hangs low in the sky. Soon it will be a myriad of blood oranges and ghostly greys.

I spot the smooth rocks where I used to play as a kid and drift down to the edge of the ocean, smelling the crisp salty air of the surf.

The black rocks off to my right call to me. I take a seat, tilt my face to the sun, and close my eyes. Once upon a time I took long walks with her here. Laughed with childhood friends as we collected seashells.

"Excuse me, Sir. Can you move?" a lilting, annoyed voice calls out.

I open my eyes and focus on the dream before me. Long brown hair, flying in the wind. Sweet, rosy lips. Eyes as blue as the ocean. Pink Wonder Woman t-shirt hugging a set of pretty wonderful tits. A body composed of tight curves with long legs flowing out from a jean mini skirt.

Her eyes narrow on me. "Well?" She gives me a little move along head gesture.

"I'm sorry?" I ask.

There's not a soul in sight, so I'm not sure why she needs me to move. Or where she even came from for that matter.

"Can you please move?" she repeats.

"No, I can't." Fuck this. Public beach. Public property.

"I asked nicely."

"Noted." I close my eyes, breathing in the saline air once again, trying my best to tune her out.

"I need that rock between your legs," she continues, apparently oblivious to my zen seeking state.

Now she's got my attention. I open my eyes. "Well, I've never been propositioned like that before. Let me get this straight, you need the 'hard rock' between my legs?" I crack a smile. "Wow, and I don't even know your name."

"It's Cat, and that rock is perfect," she says, not catching my meaning.

"I've been told that. A perfect, hard rock between my legs." I wink, grabbing my crotch with one hand. "I'm blessed in that department."

She blushes. "Not that." She shakes her head. "I mean the rock at your feet. I need it."

She needs a rock? I glance around at about five hundred other black rocks littering the beach.

"Right," I draw out. "So, Hell Cat, you need a hard rock? Please, tell me more."

"You don't understand. That one is perfect for what I'm doing." She brandishes me with a pleading stare.

"What could you possibly need a rock for?"

"A waterfall."

Her eyes sparkle when she smiles. I want to keep looking at her, but I don't.

"Well, I'm sure the other rocks will work just fine. A rock is a rock."

"You're not very nice."

I laugh as her cheeks redden with anger. "I know. Some say it's my best quality."

"Well, that's just sad." She sighs. "Let's start over. My name's Cat. I run a little business called Cat's Landscaping Creations. I'm working on a waterfall, and that rock right there," she points to one flat, black rock at my feet, "would be perfect for it. I was just coming back for it after I dropped a few off at my truck."

"Well, I'm relaxing."

Sure, I could move out of her way, but where's the fun in that? I wouldn't get to see her riled up. Watch the expressions on her face change from anger to astonishment. Isn't that what life's about? Acting and reacting?

Her blue eyes hold my brown in a stare off. I pull the rock closer with my foot. A little gasp escapes her before she turns away.

Nimble and agile, like her namesake, she climbs a few more rocks, grabbing a couple and chucking them into a pile. These aren't little rocks she's collecting, so I'm impressed at her dedication.

"Hope you can *relax* when I come for that rock," she threatens, stalking closer to me.

"What the fuck?" I ask as she marches even closer, bending at her knees to grab the rock at my feet. She tugs a little, but doesn't give up.

"If you'd just move this leg." She bumps my leg with her shoulder, and I can't help but laugh a little.

"Need help?" I glare down at her.

"Yes, would you mind?"

Her deep-aqua eyes catch mine, and she really is something else. Unlike the women back in LA with plastic faces and too much makeup, her face is fresh and bare—almost innocent. We hold each other's stare, each of us silent. It would be so easy to lift this rock out of its spot and hand it to her, hell, even take it to her car. Ask for her number. Maybe even offer to buy her a drink. Something. But, I'm paralyzed.

My lips lift into a quick smile. Raising a brow, I say, "I don't mind at all. Would you like me to unzip my shorts?"

She stands in a rush, abandoning the perfect rock. "You're an asshole."

Maybe I am. Truth is, she's irritating me. I came here for peace and quiet, and all I get is this chick talking about waterfalls and rocks.

I pick up the rock, it's kind of heavy, but nothing I can't handle with one hand, and she smiles holding out both hands as if I'm going to give it over.

Something snaps within me, and I chuck it right into the ocean.

"There ya go. Now can I get back to relaxing?"

"What did you do that for?" she almost yells at me. Her indignant eyes are wide. "You're... I can't... Ugh." She storms off, abandoning the little pile she created.

If I were in a different frame of mind, I'd chase after her. Apologize. But, I can't be bothered with some beauty I met for five minutes on the beach. Hopefully, I'll never see her again.

Hours pass. The tide creeps closer to me. Beautiful and deadly. When I can no longer take the jarring thoughts in my brain, I walk once more to the edge of the frothy water, spotting the rock I threw a few feet away. The perfect rock. Nothing's perfect.

I pick it up, brushing off a few grains of clinging sand, and carry it home.

Home. As if this place could ever be fucking home. I grab a bottle of Jim, pour a glass, yes, a glass, and settle in for a night with no power. And no sleep.

Chapter Two

Cat

This has not been my week. Three lost potential clients. I like to think of myself as an entrepreneur, building my empire, doing what it takes to become successful. That's what I tell myself as I pull my Chevy truck into the local bakery, *Pretty Pastries*, to pick up a breakfast delivery for Mr. Donovan. What I'm really doing is trying to make a place for myself in this world, and it takes money to make money. So, when the sun is barely peeking over the mist covered Redwoods on Saturday mornings, and the air is still brisk, I log into my DeliciousnessDelivered app and become Ferndale, California's breakfast bitch. You do what you have to do. My earnings are deposited directly into an account to expand my landscaping business. This morning, I overslept. So people either fended for themselves or went hungry.

"Morning, Cat," the owner greets me when I step inside.

"Hey, Susan. I'm here for a pick up."

"Let me grab what I have for him." Her petite frame disappears into the back.

The chime tinkles above the door, and a man in jeans, black tshirt, and a ball cap steps up to the glass case. The swinging door opens, and she re-emerges to slide five pink donut filled cardboard boxes embossed with 'Pretty Damn Good' on the countertop. And they are. Better than good. I spot one lone chocolate covered donut, resting amid dabs of chocolate where it's companions were plucked, and decide to rescue it from its solitude.

"What can I get you?" she asks the man.

"Chocolate glazed and a coffee," his husky voice answers, dashing my dreams.

Like I said, not my week. My sigh of disappointment is louder than I intended, and soft brown eyes land on me.

Him.

The rock thrower.

Not only did he take my rock, he has now taken my donut. Who is this thief?

"That was mine," I mutter, stepping around his tall frame, gathering all the boxes at once, so I don't have to make two trips.

His thieving hands slide in his jeans pockets. "Is this about the rock?"

So, he remembers me. Most important, he doesn't apologize.

"Thanks, Susan," I call out, ignoring him.

Before I can maneuver to hip bump open the door, an arm slides around me, pushing it open.

Rock thrower smirks at me as I brush by.

He watches as I load my truck and pull away. When he is a speck in my rearview mirror, I give him the finger.

I drop Mr. Donovan's donuts off and the kind man that he is, insists on tipping me with a glazed donut. Not chocolate, just plain, but close enough.

An hour later, I pull into the driveway of my dad's home and grab my bag of rocks. Minus the one I really wanted. As much as I wanted that rock, I wasn't about to let him see me search for it.

Vibrant blossoms—dahlia, irises, and even a jasmine bush—smile at me as I weave up the cobblestone path. I did this. I created this beauty.

Before I can raise my hand to knock on the strong, Victorian-style door, my father swings it open, his gray eyes shimmering with love. A huge smile tips the edge of his lips upward. I'm swept into his arms before I have time to smile back.

"My kitty Cat, glad you're here." He takes the bag from me as Bruno, the lovable, pit wags his black-and-white tail behind him. "Did you hire anyone to help you yet like I suggested?"

He's also still under the notion that I'm eight, not twenty-eight.

"No, dad," I tell him. "I don't mind getting dirty or doing the work."

"I know. I know." He swings the door wider, pushing Bruno aside as I enter. "Just seems like you'd want a nice, strong man helping you."

I pat Bruno on the head, rolling my eyes at my father's millionth attempt to bring in a guy to help with the labor of my fledgling landscape design business. His ulterior motives are pretty obvious—he doesn't just want a helper to lift and carry the heavy things; he wants a man to take care of me.

"Are those your work boots?" he asks.

I glance down, kick my heels together like Dorothy in *The Wizard of Oz*, and smile. "Doc Martens. I love them."

"Very you," he says, unphased by my shoe choice.

"Where's Cooper?" I inquire, following him into the sun filled kitchen.

"Out back. Waiting on you."

I walk over to the sink and give a little knock on the window above it. Cooper's dark head looks up and he rushes inside when he spots me.

"Did you get the good rocks?" he asks, overly excited, practically jumping up and down.

I point to the bulging burlap bag on the counter. "Would I let you down?"

"Nope," he says, untying the string and peeking inside.

"Why don't you get started, and I'll be out in a minute?"

Like any six-year-old, that's all the encouragement he needs to grab the bag and race outside, slamming the door behind him.

Poppy, my father's live-in girlfriend, saunters into the kitchen. "Did you hear they're putting that Jennings place on the market," She stops when she sees me. "Oh, hi, Cat." She steps closer to wrap me into a hug, then pulls back, her green eyes fixed on me. "Actually, you should be interested in this house."

"Oh, why's that?" Sure, my cottage isn't the biggest in all the land, but it suits me just fine.

She eyes my father with a conspiratorial look. "My firm says they're doing a complete remodel."

My eyes spark, ears burning for more information.

Having Poppy work as the town's leading real estate agent comes in very handy in scouting possible jobs.

"I'm listening," I say.

"Well, word is," she leans in, "the house hasn't been touched since the family lived there back in the 90's."

"I wonder why they're selling now?"

Poppy with her long dark hair, and perfect posture, flexes her hand with her long red-painted nails. "Well, it was a family: husband, wife, and their little boy. After the dad died, the mother took the kid and left town."

"Oh," I say as I listen.

"Apparently, the whole town's gossiping about the son coming back to sell it. A Booker Reed. Hmm," she muses, "I guess the mother remarried, or something."

"And the yard's a mess?"

She smiles wide. "And the yard's a mess."

I purse my lips, wondering how on Earth I can finagle my way into this remodel.

She grabs her handbag and keys, then kisses my dad's cheek. "I'll be back in a few hours after the Blaine showing." She smiles at me. "Bye, Cat."

After she's gone, my father focuses back on me. "I have a boat tour tonight. Cooper can stay with us when I'm done, if you want to go out."

Did I mention my dad is obvious? He means well. This man, with his soft, trusting eyes and graying dark hair, is a saint. Not once did he falter when a mother I was too young to remember left without looking back, leaving him alone to raise a toddler girl.

I lean against the counter. "Why are you determined to get me to go out?"

He turns from me and rummages in the fridge, avoiding my stare. "Drink?"

"Daddy? You're avoiding me."

He grabs an Evian water bottle, unscrews the cap and chugs before answering. "Well, I think it's good for you to get out. Date a little. You haven't been on a date since Austin."

"I know," I tell him. "It's not easy, and besides, I'm busy."

"You work too much. You should have some fun."

I push off the counter. "I have lots of fun.

What's so wrong with me focusing on more important things besides finding a man?"

I peer out the window at Cooper's little frame, examining and stacking stones, not wanting him to feel the disappointment of someone coming into his life and leaving.

He sets the water bottle down, crunching the thin plastic in his hand. "Don't worry, Kitty Cat, you're not your mom," he says, gently.

I sure hope to god not.

"How's business?" I ask, opting to change the subject to lighter, less soul sucking things.

"Busy," he answers. "Always busy."

"I can run more tours in my down time," I offer, emptying the sink of their breakfast dishes and loading the dishwasher. "I miss the whales."

He smiles. "Luckily the tourists in this town love them as much as you."

Tourists. I wonder if rock thrower/thief is a tourist.

Cooper peeks his brown-haired head in the back door. "You coming, Mom?"

"Sorry," I tell dad, "I've got a waterfall to build with my son."

Chapter Three

Booker

Today could be a good day. Correction, it *should* be a good day. All the right elements are there. Shining sun. Cloudless sky. Birds chirping. Air in my lungs.

I'm on the precipice of feeling half way sane, but then, reality creeps in, sinking me back down before I have a chance to claw my way out. It's been three weeks since I came here. Three long weeks of putting this house back together—sanding, painting, tiling–and it still has a long way to go.

I sit up and give my head time to adjust to the spinning downstairs guest room before padding my naked body (I'm alone, so who cares.) across the now gleaming hardwoods into the kitchen. All the visible traces of footsteps that marred the skin of the foundation are gone. New stainless-steel appliances fill the former gaping holes giving the space a pulse. It still needs new countertops, new fixtures—a priest to exorcise the ghosts. So much fucking work.

Instead of reaching for the Jim Beam, I put on a pot of coffee. Today, I have to deal with the real world and its different breed of insanity. My job. It started off as something else entirely and morphed into the ridiculousness it is today: a website—The Heartbreaker—a place where men, and sometimes women, come for advice. I write articles, answer questions, advise them in finding 'true love.' I'm a fucked up Cupid.

Most of the time, I just help guys get laid. But, who am I to judge? I only play a hand in manipulating fate, the rest is up to them. I have my own shit to deal with.

My latest jobs back in LA consisted of playing the proverbial asshole so the 'hero,' my client, could swoop in and save the girl. It's a dirty job, but somebody's gotta do it.

In this cruel world, where love is blind, men need all the help they can get.

And I'm just the man for the job.

Besides, what do I care if I break a few hearts if they just go on to find true love? That's what I tell myself, break a heart so she can meet the man of her dreams.

Don't get me wrong, most times I just hit on chicks at bars and get drinks thrown in my face. It's still up to my client to prove his worth to the girl.

Amidst the spam, I spot an email from an Austin Matthews with the subject line 'Desperate. Need Your Help' and open it up.

Heard about you from a friend, and he said you were in town. I'd like to meet and talk with you about a co-worker of mine. This is a last resort, but I feel like she's worth it. Correction, I know she's worth it. Some things you have to go the extra mile for.

I scrub a palm across my jaw. I should say no. I should, but I don't. Instead, I answer back, needing to escape the responsibilities of this god forsaken house and set a meeting for tomorrow.

The next day, I pull into an overcrowded parking lot at the diner where Austin and I agreed to meet and park my black convertible Mustang. The name Jonah's blinks in neon pink on a blue, steel and aluminum whale shaped restaurant. How do people come up with this stuff? I snap a shot and text it to my best friend, Jonah.

*If you don't hear from me
in three days, send help.*

His reply is immediate.

Playboy: *Dude, it's been three weeks.
Chelsea and I were ready to drive
up there and find your ass.
Everything ok?*

My brown eyes reflect back at me in the rearview mirror. Other than a few bloodshot lines and faint charcoal smudges, I'd say I look 'ok.' The scruff lining my jaw could use a trim, probably the dark hair peeking out from beneath my ball cap too. Nothing that's not 'ok.' But that's not what he asked. Everything, he said. He knows why I'm here and for the first time, I wish he didn't. Because now I have someone holding me accountable for the solitude I want. The urge to lift the console and take out the flask hidden inside, buzzes through my veins. My mouth waters.

Me: *Sorry, man. Been busy with the house. Gotta
run, meeting a potential client for breakfast.*

Playboy: *Call me later. The guys and I can come up and help.*

Even though I should, I don't reply. He's a good friend, a better friend than I am, but the guys driving up here is the last thing I want right now. People filter into the mouth of the diner like tiny fish being swallowed up, and I follow.

Austin said he'd be wearing a Wells ORCAstrated Tours tshirt. I spot him by a window in the bowels of this mammoth restaurant. He's a brute of a man. Square shoulders, bulky arms and legs, solid neck, leading up to a chiseled jaw. He's all geometric shapes and colors—blue eyes, every shade of blonde and brown mixed in his hair that topples a little past his ears, and a few freckles to match.

He shakes my hand with a firm grip and looks me directly in the eyes. A slightly crooked smile when he laughs, but other than that he seems ok. Maybe even a little nice. We exchange awkward pleasantries about our mutual friend, he was an old client, and I order a coffee from the waitress.

"So, tell me the problem," I begin.

"A girl I've dated before wants nothing to do with me. She's great… she's smart as a whip… pretty too." He stops.

"But…"

The coffees arrive and we take a few seconds to garnish them the way we like. One cream, two sugars for me. Just three packets of sugar for Austin.

After he stirs his coffee a moment, he resumes, "Maybe I'm too nice. She friendzoned me."

Ah, the kiss of death. I don't tell him that, though. "Why do you think that?"

He shrugs. "Well, everything was going great, so I don't know."

I mull over his words, scratching the scruff along my jawline. "Have you asked her?"

He laughs, his eyes lighting to a softer shade of blue. "No, every time I get the chance, her father comes around." He points to his tee. "He owns the whale tour company. When she's not digging around in people's yards, she works part-time for him."

"So, you want me to meet her, be an asshole and what? She'll come running back to you?"

He leans forward. "Yeah, pretty much."

I take a sip of the hot coffee. "Hmm."

"Listen, just think about it. I can offer a lot of money. I'm willing to pay triple."

Lots of money to sink in the house so I can unload it and get the hell out of here sounds good right about now. "Convince me."

He nods at my answer. "I just really want her back. I think she's perfect for me."

"Yeah, but are you perfect for her?"

"I think so."

The sincerity in his tone makes me want to believe him, but I'm a cynic. "Email me everything you can about her. I'll let you know."

"Deal." Austin beams. "Here's a few pictures. Her name's Catherine Wells."

I grab the photos Austin has laid on the table.

It's her.

The girl from the beach.

The 'hard rock' girl.

"Forget the email, I'll do it."

Chapter Four

Cat

Craaaaaack. Blue glass shatters into tiny shards beneath my hammer. With precision, I cut the last few jagged pieces and push them into the mortar on the round table, finishing the azalea pattern for Mrs. Dennis. This is my favorite part of what I do: creating mosaic works of art that have a special meaning to the client. When she asked for the table, I knew exactly what design I would make for her.

I snap a few pictures as Mrs. Dennis rounds the corner. Her blue eyes fill with tears when she sees what I've made.

"It's beautiful," she says, softly. "Harold loved azaleas."

I give her a hug. "Now you'll have them year round. I'll be back in a few days to finish it. I just need to let it set before I apply the grout."

"It doesn't even look like the same space," she marvels, walking across the paver stones that now form her own private retreat. Plants that will bloom seasonally line the new circular patio, ensuring she will always have something pretty to look at. "I love this," she beams, taking a seat on the bench semi-circling her new fire pit.

We settle the hefty bill, and on the way home I grab a pizza for Cooper and wine for me.

"Hey," Poppy greets me, when I walk in the door. She takes the large pizza box from me and slides it on the island.

"How was he? Did he get his homework done?" I ask, setting my purse on the counter alongside the pizza.

"He was fine."

I stare into her kind face and nod. "Thanks, for watching him. Pizza?"

"No, I'm going to head home and make dinner." She walks toward the front door, glancing back over her shoulder. "Did you hear anything about that Jennings place?"

I bite my lower lip. "No, not yet."

"I listed you as a recommendation." She winks on her way out the door, and I cross my fingers hoping I get the job.

After Cooper and I scarf down pizza and watch a little TV, I update my website with the latest pictures of Mrs. Dennis's yard.

This was a big job, and now, if I could get more people in Ferndale to need more than flowers planted, I'd be doing okay. Starting a new business is hard, much harder than I expected. Especially in a small town like Ferndale.

Once Cooper is in bed, I change into sleep shorts and a tank and climb in bed with my laptop. A new job request has come through, and I open the email, hoping it's the Jennings place.

Hello,

I'm in the process of completing renovations on a home I'm selling. Your name was given to me regarding an overhaul in the backyard. When I say overhaul, I mean there's virtually nothing but dead weeds and a concrete slab. I'd like to set up a consultation.

Booker Reed

I answer back immediately. Something this extensive would be at the top of my nearly nonexistent portfolio. In the next few hours, he responds with a meeting time and his address, and I do a little jump for joy in my head as I think about bringing the Jenning's backyard to life.

Two days later, I pull into Mr. Reed's driveway and take a deep breath before getting out. The house is a bit intimidating, definitely in need of some tender loving care, but still beautiful. In true Ferndale Victorian-style, it looks like a gingerbread house on steroids. Spiers point to the blue sky and grand columns line the wraparound porch. But, the best part is the bright yellow trim. Looks like frosting.

I head up the drive and ring the bell.

No answer.

I knock.

Five minutes later, still no answer. After double checking that I didn't mix up the date or time, I decide to sneak a look at the back yard and follow the weathered boards around to the back of the house. I hop off the side, slip through the grass and round the corner to a view that can only be described as breathtaking. No, not the ocean, although, that's magnificent as well. A man, dark haired, tall and lean, with muscles etched into his flat stomach, stands completely *nude* inside the open patio door, pouring coffee into a mug. He looks over at me and is the epitome of cool, standing there with a cocky smile, gazing down on me like he doesn't have a care in the world. It's the type of smile that can make a girl like me forget he threw my...

It only takes a few seconds for the recognition to hit.

"No way," I whisper before turning and hightailing it to my truck.

"Wait," he calls out.

But I don't. Nude man, Booker Reed, donut thief, the guy who callously threw my rock into the ocean, races after me. He grabs my arm, spinning me around. A red dishtowel covers his impressive junk.

"Oh my god, you're naked," I exclaim. "In your driveway," I tell him, since he doesn't seem to realize this.

"Let's start over," he says in a throaty whisper.

"Let's not, Mr. Reed." I wiggle free from his hold and open my truck door.

"Please, call me Booker. I'm sorry about the other day."

I cross my arms, weakening a little at the sheepish look on his face. "Oh yeah?"

He drops his head. "Yes, Catherine."

The use of my full name disarms me. No one really uses it. I'm Cat or Kitty Cat, always some type of feline. Hearing Catherine fall from his lips is unexpected and a little unnerving; it makes me feel like a woman, not a little girl pretending to be an adult.

"You were a jerk."

"Well, you were a bit annoying that day," he clips out.

"Me? Well I guess I'm annoying every day if being polite is your measure of annoying."

He holds up a hand, the other still holding the towel covering himself, and takes a step back. "Fine, I guess I'll take my business elsewhere?"

I bite my lower lip. I really want this job. The ideas in my head are already more than my brain can process. And I do need the money. The payment I earn will cover expenses for months. Life is about dealing with people and behaviors you don't necessarily like and adapting. I've learned this the hard way. So, I give in a little and test the waters. "If I take this job, I won't have to deal with you, will I?"

In one fell swoop, he splashes the water back in my face. "Believe me, I don't want to deal with you either." He turns and strolls toward the front door, his muscular ass in full sight. "I don't want to deal with anybody," he mumbles.

Ugh. I already know deep within my soul I'm going to take this job. This is business and not the same as walking away from a rock rather than give him the satisfaction of seeing me retrieve it. It's the accepting it from him; I don't like that part. Letting him know he has this power over me, because of my want of a job, is not going to be fun to admit. But, I have more than myself to think about.

"Wait," I call out to the corded muscles rippling in his back. "Show me the yard again. I'll draw up a design, and if you even like my ideas, then you can hire me, I guess."

He stops, turns, meeting my eyes. "You guess?"

I shrug. "Yeah, who knows if you will even like what I have to offer."

His eyes rake over me, lazy and roguish, starting at my feet, up to my breasts, lingering on my lips, then meeting my eyes. "I'm pretty sure I'll like what you have to offer."

This is the second time he's flustered me to the point of blushing. "Well, you know what I mean."

He opens the door and waits for me to join him. "I do know what you mean," he whispers close to the shell of my ear as I pass.

The scent of fresh paint lingers in the air when I step past the marble entryway.

"Besides, who says I'll like what you have to offer."

"Well that's just laughable," he counters. "Of course, you won't like it." His voice drops. "You'll love it."

I'm not going to win this sexual innuendo war with him, if that's what this is. I'm unarmed, and his dick is big enough to slay a nation. So, I ignore the predatory gleam in his eye. I'm sure this guy has no problem finding girls who will drop to their knees in awe of his 'charm.'

"Give me five minutes," he says, disappearing down a hallway, as if it's perfectly normal we had an entire conversation while he's naked.

I step further into the large living area admiring the woodwork. This house has a lot of character, much more than my little cottage. Crown moldings accent the high ceilings and open floor plan littered with drop cloths and tools of a renovation.

His footsteps echo as he crosses back into the main room, dressed in jeans and no shirt. Maybe he doesn't own full outfits. Honestly, I wouldn't blame him. His body is beautiful.

He pulls back the large curtain. "These will be replaced with blinds, so whatever you do will be visible from here," he explains, but I'm no longer listening.

In the distance, the ocean waves crash against the rocks blocking it's path. A spray of disapproval that anything dare impede its course mists in the air. I study the majesty of it all. Beautiful calamity. Now that I've seen this view, a few of my ideas have changed. The ocean is the star here. Everything else is only a supporting character in place to make it shine.

"Let's go out back," he says, and I follow him through the open slider. A breeze brushes past me bringing with it his cologne.

A huge western hemlock stands proud in one corner of the lot, with low-hanging branches and lots of attitude. Sword ferns and sorrel grace a corner of the space, and I smile in excitement at the possibilities.

"Booker?" I ask, ready to dazzle him.

"Yeah." He stands so close I lose my train of thought for a moment.

"Booker, I think I have some ideas you'll love."

Again, he smiles. A smile so infectious it makes me join in. It's dangerous. *He's* dangerous. The type of man who would make me break all my rules.

Chapter Five

Booker

Walking through the backyard with this sexy little thing, is excruciatingly hard. The breeze lifts her flowy top giving me a tantalizing glimpse of her stomach.

"And over here you can brighten up the shady spots with a few rose bushes." She's so animated, I'm almost fucking excited listening to her ideas about transforming this dump into something special.

As she leads me to different areas of the yard, she stops and runs a pink tipped nail briskly against her bottom lip then gives it a little tap before spewing her visions. It's as if the motion stops the wheel spinning in her brain. She's intriguing. Maybe even someone I would pursue in different circumstances.

"So, you think this place is fixup-able?" I ask, leaning up against the knobby trunk of a tree.

"Have you been listening to anything I've said?" she asks, seeming slightly perturbed.

She's going to be a handful. Whether or not I'm up for this challenge remains to be seen. And that excites me more than I care to admit.

"I'm sorry. What did you say?" I deadpan.

Glints of red in her brown hair escape from the loose braid trying to contain them, swirling around her face like sparks of anger. "Are you always so difficult? Because, honestly, maybe I'm not a good fit for you."

"Oh, I'm sure you'd be a good fit," I say, letting my eyes drift to her pussy hidden beneath little navy shorts.

"Booker," she snaps, making a V with her fingers, pointing at the twin blue slits narrowed on me. "My vagina isn't speaking to you. I am. Eyes up here, please."

I smirk. As irritated as she obviously is, and she is, she threw a 'please' on the end. Polite fury. Mad enough to call me out but still *nice*. Lashing out and then kissing away the sting.

"Why don't we go inside and discuss things?" I turn away from her and close the distance to the patio.

"Is this more innuendo?" she asks, following behind me.

"Innuendo?" I lead her to the small thrift store purchased breakfast table.

"Nevermind."

She slides into the wooden chair opposite me. Her eyes dart from mine, like a precarious game of cat and mouse.

"So," I lean forward, resting my forearms on the nicked oak table, "where do you see yourself in five years?"

Cat connects her fingers, like two lovers holding hands and rests her elbows on the table. "I don't know. Here, in Ferndale?"

"I'm teasing, Catherine," I tell her. "You don't get my sense of humor at all, do you?"

"Oh, is that what it is?" She closes her eyes briefly, then leans forward, palms splayed on the table. Her hands look too small, too soft, to do the task in the backyard. "Can I be honest with you?"

This should be interesting. Most women are flirting with me by now, Catherine isn't. For the first time since I arrived here, I feel the oppressing weight lift in anticipation of what she's going to say. "Sure."

"I can forgive you for taking my rock and my donut…"

"Wait, what?" I cut in. "Your donut?"

"Yes. I had claimed that last chocolate donut in my mind. Anyways, I don't like to carry grudges, it's bad for the soul. I want this job," she pauses a moment, "so I think we can work together."

I nod. "I think we can too, Catherine."

She smiles, sweet, unassuming, and I see why Austin is captivated by her. "Great. What's the timeline?" she asks.

"A few months, maybe. A realtor is stopping by later this afternoon to give me an opinion."

She nods, glancing around the kitchen. "So, you're living here until it sells?"

"Yeah."

I brace myself for an onslaught of curiosity about things I don't want to answer, but she rises, leaving unasked questions in the air. "Okay, I'll email you an estimate and we can go from there."

"Good."

I follow her to the door.

"Nice meeting you, Booker," she says, glancing over her shoulder. She leaves, taking with her the sunshine. How utterly metaphoric. Fat gray clouds swell across the sky.

I sit in the kitchen for who knows how many hours.

The house is empty.

Empty like me.

I will myself to snap into work mode and end up updating my website for a bit then write an article.

A zap fires in my chest when I see Cat has sent over her plans for the backyard.

I barely even look at them, it's all jibberish to me anyways, before typing my reply

Yes.

I hammer out the details, agreeing on her proposed fee. She'll start this weekend. I'm only a pawn helping open her eyes, those clear blue eyes, to what guys can be like, I tell myself.

My friends would say that's a lame ass excuse. Fuck. My friends.

Truth is, I've been neglecting them since I came here.

I call Jonah, waiting for him to pick up.

"Booker, my man. How's the house?"

"It's definitely a project." My low voice sports a hint of desolation to my own ears.

Jonah picks up on it immediately. "Maybe you need a break." He clears his throat. "Come back to LA for a night or two. Clear your head."

"Well, I picked up a job here."

Before I can get out anything about the job, Jonah cuts in, "She hot?"

I take a deep breath, letting it out slowly. "She's different."

All laughter is gone from his voice when he answers with a single 'oh.'

"What? I just mean she's not like the girls in LA."

Jonah remains silent, and I ask him 'what' a few times.

"Do you like her?" he asks.

"No," I scoff. "Of course not. I barely know her. And, I've never fallen for a client before."

"You've never fallen for anyone."

"And I'd like to keep it that way," I finish off.

"Whoa, calm down. I know it can't be easy…" his voice trails off.

Jonah has been my best friend for years. Actually, when I left this town and moved to LA, Jonah was the first kid I met.

We were both ten. I was a lanky boy at a new school, and Jonah walked right up to me and introduced himself. I met Declan and Ethan hours later at lunch.

We've been close ever since. They were there for me through my darkest days. We catch up on a few things—his job at *Bunny Hunnies*, his wife, Chelsea—and after I hang up, I change into track shorts and my running shoes to release the energy before I fucking blow.

I set off, one foot in front of the other, in a slow jog.

The crisp evening air fills my lungs with each deep breath I take.

Each step becomes faster than the one before. I'm in a full-on sprint, racing to nowhere. Just away. I round the edge of the neighborhood and spot a little coffee/bait shop. Catching my breath, I bend over, hands on my knees, and let myself calm down. This will be easy. Nothing to fear, I tell myself.

A bell dings over my head as I step inside the quiet store.

The gray-haired hippie behind the counter looks up at me. "Hey, if you need any help…" his voice trails off, and I wonder if he needs another hit of weed to restart. It's obvious this guy's a stoner.

"Thanks," I say, moving around the store.

He steps away from the white laminate counter, his eyes trained on me. "Haven't seen you around here before."

My pulse starts a steady rhythm, the blood whooshing in my ears. "Yeah, I'm just in town for a few months." I take a step toward the door.

His bloodshot eyes hold questions his pot-warped mind can't fully express. "Where you staying?"

"Up the road."

"That so?"

"It is." I need to bail, but he's so close to me now I can smell the corn chips he was munching on when I first stepped inside.

"You're not staying at that old Jennings place, are you?" He steps closer. "Wait, are you…"

Before he can finish, I'm out the door, running as fast as I can. Back to the Jennings place.

Chapter Six

Cat

I pull the rope tighter, securing the boat on the dock.

"Cat, how was it today?" Austin asks from behind me, leaning in to give a forceful tug to the rope.

"It was good. We had to cut it short with the storm heading in."

Austin's blue eyes peer up at the looming dark clouds.

"A few of us are hanging out tonight at Old Miller's Pub. Want to come?"

This isn't the first time he's asked me to join them. Austin is fairly new to my dad's business, six months or so, and he seems like an alright guy. Once or twice, I went to dinner with him when he first started.

He's the type of guy I could see having a relationship with and maybe even marrying. But, I don't see the excitement of a grand love affair. He's just normal, I guess. Safe.

I don't see the magic and mystery of him sweeping me off my feet or the words madly in love playing a part in our relationship.

But, maybe that stuff isn't real. Maybe it's just something made up. Something the movies and fairy tales of the world want us to believe in. Since that, the few times a month I run a tour, I've mostly seen him in passing, ten-minute conversations here and there. So far, he hasn't sank a boat, so dad seems happy with him.

Usually, I politely decline, but maybe I do need some fun. Cooper is spending the night at dad's, so hanging out with everyone from work sounds much better than sitting home and trying to pretend I'm not nervous about heading out to Booker's place tomorrow. It's Friday night, and I'm young and child free for the night. Why not?

"Sure," I agree.

For a moment, he appears stunned, and then, a smile spreads. "Cool. Meet up at eight?"

"Perfect."

He gives me a larger than necessary grin, and I feel the need to either amp up my smile or escape. "I'm just going to lock up," I tell him, opting for escape. "See ya later."

He appears thunderstruck and gives me a chin nod, still grinning. I cross the street to the Wells ORCAstrated Tours building, complete the days paperwork and head home to shower and change.

Two hours later, dressed in skinny jeans and an off the shoulder white blouse, I pull up to the marina ready to have a few drinks and take the edge off.

I spot my best friend, Tristan, and an old friend from school, Eli, hanging out near the front door of the tavern.

"Hey, guys," I call out, smiling as I approach them.

Eli holds the door open, and we slip inside. I like this place. It's all wood decks and sits right on the beach with a rustic nautical theme. Anchors weigh down the tables and masts flutter in the breeze. All that's missing is Jack Sparrow.

Tristan grabs my arm, pulling me closer to whisper in my ear, "Do not let me throw myself at Eli. Alcohol makes me do crazy things."

I glimpse over at Eli and smile at Tristan. She's sweet with long brown hair and large hazel doe eyes, and trying to hide a crush so epic it makes me feel bad for her. "I'll do my best."

We head off in the direction of the bar and spot Mikey, the bartender, pushing drinks and smiling to the guests sitting on wood stools. He looks up and waves.

"Beers or girly drinks?" Eli asks.

"Beer," we both answer.

He winks. "Good choice."

Tristan and I grab a seat at a nearby table.

"Panty alert," I warn, after she flashes me.

"Damn it," she tugs down the short, red dress that looks stunning on her, "I knew I shouldn't have worn this."

"Maybe you should've worn a longer dress," Eli says, sliding our beers on the table. He chews the silver ring in his bottom lip. "What color are they?"

"What color is what?" Austin asks, taking a seat.

"My new... chairs," Tristan answers, quickly. "They're red."

Eli takes a long pull of his beer, eyeing her. It's been so long since I've been out, it's like I'm watching a documentary on mating rituals.

An easy conversation settles over the table about everyone's work week, and while I'm not necessarily bored, maybe just a little too preoccupied about tomorrow, I don't feel like joining in. Maybe I don't know how to interact with adults anymore. No one is dropping a crayon under the table or needs their mouth wiped, so I'm unsure of what to do with myself. My eyes shift to the ocean, the waves barely cresting along the shore. The full moon hangs low in the sky, its shadow skating across the water.

"Cat, what about you?" Austin asks, holding his beer an inch away from his lips.

I shake my head. "I'm sorry. What was the question?"

Tristan rolls her eyes. "They want to know your favorite sexual position."

My expression blanks. "Why?"

"Oh, come on, we've all shared ours," Austin says.

I clear my throat. "I guess the standard position."

Honestly, I wouldn't have a clue as to what position I like best. My sexual experience isn't outlandish; I've only ever been with two guys. Neither was that great or often, and one of them resulted in Cooper. Gavin was a tourist passing through Ferndale, taking a whale tour, and I was a twenty-one-year-old girl who got lost in the moment, never expecting to end up pregnant by a guy who signed all his rights away because it would ruin his future. Still, I can't say it was a mistake, like Gavin did, because then Cooper would be a mistake. I muster up a fake smile and take another sip of beer.

Austin beams. "The standard position? What kind of answer is that?" he presses.

I shrug. "It's a good answer."

"I agree," Tristan says, raising her beer to clink it with mine in a cheers.

I smile, glad she's taking my side. Girl solidarity. And besides, even if I fucked hanging from the ceiling, what's it to him?

I'm formulating my excuse to leave when something down by the shore catches my eye.

A man, strolling down by the sea, stumbling around. I stand and move closer to the edge of the deck, holding on to the light-wood pillar.

He turns, facing me, and... it's Booker.

The moonlight illuminates his features. A thick curiosity washes over me, so heavy as it cascades around me, spinning my mind out of control.

What's he doing?

I glimpse back at the table with my friends, happily chatting away.

A snap decision is made, probably a rash one, if anyone is keeping score, and I rush back to the table, grab my purse and smile. "Guys, I'm gonna take off."

"Are you sure?" Austin asks, rising from his seat.

"Yes. Early day tomorrow." After quick good nights, I make my way to the stairs leading down to the beach.

I slip my shoes off and plod through the cool sand. "Booker?" I call out, approaching from behind as he stares out at the frothy waves.

He turns to me, stumbling a bit. "Cat? Is that you?" He grabs my shoulders, and leans down to glare directly into my eyes. The stout smell of bourbon envelopes me.

"Are you drunk?"

"Are you?"

"Uh, no. Maybe I should get you home."

He teeters closer. "Maybe I should get *you* home."

"Oh, you're like my little echo." I laugh.

He wraps an arm around me wearing a big goofy grin. But, in the light of the moon his eyes don't match the smile; they're lifeless. The quote from *Jaws* sounds in my head: " 'And you know the thing about a shark… he's got lifeless eyes. Black eyes. Like a doll's eyes.' "

A shiver courses through me.

"Do you know it only takes a second? Like a grain of sand." He grabs a handful of sand, nearly crashing us to the ground. "Look at this sand, it was only a second." He drops the sand, wiping the remnants off on his jeans.

I have no clue as to what he's hammering on about, but I have creeped myself the fuck out. I just nod, leading him up the coast toward his house. He staggers back a little, his eyes blink slow and heavy as if it's all he can do to keep them open.

"Listen, don't face plant on me in the sand," I tell him.

He stops. I fear he might fall by the way he sways toward me. I put a hand on his solid chest to steady him, and his eyes drop down to stare at it.

"You're touching me," he whispers.

"I'm just trying to keep you from falling flat on your face."

He chuckles at that. "You're funny."

"Thanks, big guy, let's go."

I drape his arm around me, sliding my arm around his waist. We plod along the sand in the silence of the night. No sounds except his breathing. Even the waves lap quietly on the shore as if they are watching and waiting to see if I succeed in getting him home.

It's odd being this close to him. I don't even know him. And what I do know, I don't particularly like. At all. Except maybe his looks. Ok, it's superficial, I know, but the man is like a movie star. Like his looks should come with their own zip code.

"Can I ask you something?"

I stop walking. "Sure."

"Will you help me?" His earnest tone tugs at my heartstrings, and without questioning, I nod in agreement.

We walk back to the house in silence. Every once in awhile Booker laughs.

He trips over nothing.

Laugh.

He stumbles up his front walkway.

Laugh.

He can't figure out where his keys are.

Laugh.

Once I finally get him inside, it's as though I've walked a hundred miles.

"Which room's yours?"

"Guess," he slurs. "If you guess the right door, you win the prize, Hell Cat."

I roll my eyes and drag him down the hall. There's no way I can even think about getting him up the stairs, so I don't try. Hopefully one of these doors is a bedroom.

I open the first door—bathroom—and then shut it. "Bzzzz," he says, "wrong door."

"It would be much more helpful if you actually helped."

"Caaat," he drawls out.

"Yes?"

His shoulder hits the wall in a drunken stumble. "Please, help me." The pleading tone is back, and I gaze into his eyes. So mysterious. So melancholy. So lost.

A niggle of intuition that something isn't quite right here, that he wasn't drinking himself into this stupor to just have a good time, sets anxious butterflies alight in the pit of my stomach. "I am helping you," I whisper back.

"No."

I stare blankly at him. "Ok." I open a few more doors. Linen closet. Laundry room. Another freaking closet.

Finally, I open a door to a bedroom. Hallelujah. I've struck gold. This room actually appears lived in. The bed isn't much, and as I help him into it, he seems so childlike.

Innocent.

A boy lost in the world. A ludicrous urge to protect him emerges.

But, then, I remember how he is when he's sober—crass, cold, and cranky. He doesn't need me to protect him.

I flip on the bedside table lamp and pull the slate gray comforter up higher against his body.

Unable to resist, I brush back an errant strand of dark hair from his forehead.

"You should sleep this off," I tell him in a soft, comforting voice.

He grabs my arm. "Cat, I need you." His eyes seem cognizant for the first time tonight.

I've never had a man say those words to me before, and an unfamiliar ache ignites in my center.

"I'll be here in the morning to start working."

"No, I need you now."

The ache gets stronger. Even though I like the way he says he needs me, the fact of the matter is: he's drunk. And he probably doesn't even mean it in a sexual way. Probably.

Besides, I'm not interested in sex with him. I can tell my mind that all day long, but my body has other reactions to his neediness—it turns me on. I haven't been turned on in a very long time.

I'm almost falling for it, almost have the urge to strip down bare. I shake my head. No.

I lean closer, intoxicated by his desperation. "What do you need?"

He strokes my cheek, and I hold my breath. "Make me come," he says and then passes out.

I.

Can't.

Breathe.

I stand on shaky legs and run.

Out of his house.

Down the beach, back to my car and head home.

How am I supposed to face him tomorrow?

The words echo through my mind all night long.

Make me come.

Chapter Seven

Booker

My head feels like someone smashed it with a sledgehammer. I reek of booze and bad choices. Foggy memories of the previous night flutter through my mind, fading in and out. Cat. Stumbling home. Unable to discern between reality and fantasy, I roll out of bed.

Did I even see Catherine last night?

Was she really here?

Or, like all the other ghosts of my past, was she merely a figment of my own fucked up imagination?

I shower, and like I do every morning, make my way to the kitchen completely nude. It's a primal ritual, telling the dictatorial society who says I have to dress before having my coffee to fuck off.

"Holy shit," I bark out.

Cat, dressed in a Batgirl tee and tiny denim shorts, stands next to the kitchen counter, scooping coffee into a filter.

"Shiiiiiiiit," she yells back at me, jumping. Coffee scatters on the countertop like scurrying ants.

Her stricken eyes skirt over every muscle on my body, lingering on my semi-erect cock. It pulses the entire time her eyes are on it. I don't try to cover him up. Let her see.

She blushes and opens her mouth to speak, then stops.

I've left her speechless. "Cat got your tongue?"

She covers her eyes. "Will you put that thing away?"

"Thing?" I grin at her discomfort. "My perfect hard rock, Cat?"

"Yes, please put it away."

"Not until you tell me why you're standing in my kitchen."

"We start today," she explains, "and I wanted to check on you. You were pretty wasted last night. I was worried."

Her answer surprises me. Worried. She was worried. About someone she doesn't even know. About some dick who threw her rock in the ocean and stole her fucking donut. About some asshole playing god with people's fate.

I don't want her to be so nice—so pretty. Remaining detached is how I've always operated, and that's how it needs to be.

"Let me get dressed." I head down the hall, calling out over my shoulder, "And relax, you act like you've never seen one before."

When I return, the mess is cleaned and the strong aroma of coffee permeates the air.

"I'm heading to the nursery," she informs me, holding out a silver travel mug. "You're coming with me. You can pick out what you like."

"You do remember I'm selling the place, right? Doesn't matter what I like." I grin, leaning against the counter.

"Well, you can still have a say." Her voice wavers between nice and short. It's like she doesn't know how to act around me.

And I don't blame her one fucking bit.

With the way I have been toward her, I'm surprised she's being civil at all.

Against my better judgment, I decide to play nice. I take the coffee mug and grab my keys. "Let's go."

We hop in my mustang and put the top down. She smiles, not caring the wind is turning her hair into a mini tornado around her head. It's sexy.

She navigates me to the local nursery, and when we step inside, greenery assaults my eyes from every corner of the massive warehouse building.

"They have the best selection of plants around," she tells me, waving at a girl behind the counter. Another employee waves as we pass, and I feel really out of place.

"You're quite popular here."

"I like to shop."

"Most girls like to shop for clothes not plants."

"I guess I'm not like most girls, then."

"No, Catherine, you most definitely are not."

We weave through the pallets covering the concrete floor. Plants. Plants. Plants. Of every shape and color. Boring. I can't even pretend to try to be interested. But, anything is better than sitting at home alone.

I get enough of that at night.

Being around Cat today, and out of the house, I have to say, my mood has shifted.

The deep dark despair has lifted a bit, leaving in its wake a soft, shimmering ray of hope. Now I just need to hold onto it. Not let it go.

Because if it leaves me, if it fades out, then I'll have nothing left but the darkness again. And I don't like that.

I don't like where my head is at when the darkness washes over me.

So, instead, I walk around a nursery, glancing at plants. Plants I don't give two shits about. But, Cat does.

I hope Austin appreciates her love of plants.

Who am I kidding? Of course he does. He thinks he loves her.

I've never loved anyone.

And that scares the ever-loving shit out of me. No love. No pain. No feeling whatsoever.

What do they call people who don't feel?

Exactly.

Psychopath.

And that's not me.

No, it's not me.

My shrink would be proud I'm analyzing my inner psyche while looking at fucking potted plants. I should pull over a lawn chair, really have a go at it. She says I feel too much.

She might be right, because I feel that if I stand here next to Cat for a second longer, I may just kiss her. I'm not sure why my mind went there with her. But, she's got these great lips. Her lips are what sonnets are written about. I'm sure Shakespeare had a girl just like her.

One who smiled at flowers.

A girl who smelled even sweeter.

I'm sure he had a girl just like her.

And those lips will be my undoing unless I remember why she's around in the first place.

She's meant to be with another man.

"What do you think of these?" her sweet voice sounds.

She holds up a potted plant, green leaves with red buds.

I nod. "Ok, sure."

"Do you really like them?" She arches a brow.

I scrub a hand down my face. "Yeah."

"Hmm, really?"

"Honestly? They all look the fucking same to me."

I roll my eyes and turn away.

"You don't have to be a jerk," she calls to my back.

"I said I liked them," I call back over my shoulder.

"I shouldn't have brought you along," she mumbles.

"I heard that."

"Good."

I keep walking away from her, down the aisle, the reds, yellows, and purples of each flower catching my eyes as I pass by. I wander into an area filled with garden statues and gnomes. Creepy little fuckers.

"Can I help you?" a lady with a short grey bob, asks.

"Just browsing."

She slides her hands in the pockets of her red smock. "You're here with Cat?"

"That I am." I pick up a small stone statue of two turtles humping, inscribed with 'Faster. Faster." This definitely needs to be in the garden.

"She's great."

So I've heard.

"She said she's working for you, fixing up the backyard because you're selling." I snap my eyes over at her. "Always loved that house. Your parents were good people. How's your mom?"

"Dead," I tell her.

"Oh, I'm sorry to hear that," she sympathizes, her thin pink lips tilted down.

Well, that's enough of this.

It makes me moody and broody. Bothered and twitchy. A headache works its way into my temples, squeezing, and I no longer want to be here.

"Thanks." I take my turtle and walk away.

Unable to find Cat in this maze of green, I spot one of those phone paging things on a pillar.

Aggravated, I pick it up. "Attention, please," my deep voice sounds across the space, "Catherine Wells, wherever you are, tear yourself away and report to the tiki torch aisle. Stat."

Two minutes later, she rounds the corner, an invoice in her hand.

"Seriously?" she says, her tits bouncing beneath her tee. "I was placing an order."

"Didn't your mom ever tell you not to wander off?"

She stops in her tracks, a shadow of hurt passing over her features. "Actually, no. But maybe someone should've told her, considering she left a little girl and never came back."

"Shit, I'm sorry."

She shakes her head. "It's ok," she says, trying to make me feel better. "I'm not bitter, even though I may sound it."

I can't help it, I smile. And then she smiles back, slow and easy, and just like that the tension in my head eases.

"I picked something out," I tell her, holding out the turtles.

She steps closer and laughs. "That's probably the slowest sex there is."

Suddenly, it's a thousand degrees in here—a hothouse rather than a nursery. Man is one of life's simplest creatures, letting the one thing we know for certain drive us in everything we do...sex.

It's true. Research says men think about sex on average about nineteen times a day. Some even say they think about it every seven seconds. If that's the case, it's over eight-thousand times a day in sixteen waking hours. And now, thanks to her innocent remark, her sweet smell, slow, unhurried sex with Cat rushes through my mind. Her begging me to go faster.

She looks up at me, her eyes drifting across my face, dropping to my lips. Instinctively, I lick them.

"Cash register is up front," she says, turning away.

When we return to the house, I help her unload potting soil and mulch. This shit is heavy, and I'm not sure how a petite girl like Cat manages this stuff by herself.

"First thing I need to do is clear the area," she states, hands on hips, surveying the yard.

"Clear the area?" She looks over at me. "That sounds very ominous."

"Don't be scared. I'm a professional," she reassures me, with a twinkle in her eye. "A stick of dynamite and we're good to go."

"Actually, that's not a bad idea," I say. "Blow the whole place up. Then I won't have to feel guilty."

She tilts her head, and the quizzical look on her face tells me I should've kept my mouth shut. I've spent years constructing these walls, and in one day, Catherine Wells knocked a hole in one.

I slap my hands together. "Let's get started."

"Well no," she says. "The client doesn't help me."

"Well I'm not the normal client."

"I'll say," she murmurs.

And for the remainder of the day that's what we do. Together. Silent. Working, sweating, moving as one to clear every last bush, weed, and dying shrub from the yard. Ripping the clinging roots from their home.

A good first day. A good distraction.

"I'll be back tomorrow," she says, removing her work gloves.

A smidge of dirt streaks her cheekbone. Without thinking, I thumb it away. Her skin is soft, tempting.

"I promise I'll be dressed," I say, dropping my hand. Then I let the asshole out. "Unless you don't want me to be."

She gives me nothing in return. "Be dressed, please."

Please. Again with the please instead of telling me to choke on my own dick. After she leaves, I head to my computer. Google.

A quick search on Catherine Wells shows me everything I want to know.

But I don't care about any of that. One goal. I have one goal. I click on images and am relieved when I see her face.

Breathing heavily, I unzip my jeans and pull my already hard cock out and jerk off to thoughts of her.

There's nothing gentle about how I handle myself.

Fuck her for turning me on with her niceness.

Fuck her delicate curves and soft skin.

I stroke my cock imagining kissing her rosy lips, massaging those round, plump breasts, squeezing her ass and making her moan in pleasure.

My cock grows painfully hard, and there's only one thing that will ease the torture: release. I want to touch her, run my fingers through her slippery heat.

Ah, it feels so good.

My cock throbs. My balls tighten.

My mind races.

Once I come so hard I can barely breathe, I grab the bottle of bourbon. Fuck a glass.

I clean myself up, and then down as much as I can in one giant gulp.

I keep drinking until I can't see straight. Until the image of Catherine is erased from my head. Until the smell of her sweet perfume is gone.

Until I can't physically stand up and function.

And then I drink a little more as I curse out loud.

Fuck this house.

Fuck this life that was handed to me.

And fuck Austin for bringing this girl to me.

Chapter Eight

Cat

"Need some help?" Eli, asks. Booker hired him a week ago to rewire some of the rooms, and it's been nice having a familiar face around. His black work boots, the same color as his hair, stop at the perimeter of the new patio.

On my hands and knees, I wiggle the last four by four paver stone into place. I look up at him, shading my eyes from the bright sun. "Nope, I'm good."

He bites at the ring in his lip, his blue eyes meeting mine. "You're moving pretty fast on this."

"Yeah, I'm ahead of schedule."

I rise and stretch out the kinks in my muscles and then glance into the kitchen. No sign of him. He was nude again this morning, and it's all I can think about. Dig a hole—think about his chiseled stomach. Plant a bush—think about the fine line of hair running from beneath his belly button to his manscaping. He kept his initial promise. For two weeks, actually, he did. Now that he has workers coming in and out, well two—Eli, and Blake, the plumbing guy—he can't be strutting about naked. But today I arrived early, and got the full view again. The first time was definitely a shock to my system.

So much flesh.

So many inches of flesh.

So. Many. Inches.

Like he wanted me to see him.

Well, mission accomplished, I saw him alright.

The patio door slides open and Booker looks between us.

"Hey, man," Eli greets him. "I'm headed out. I'll be back tomorrow to install the light fixtures. You should bring Cat with you to pick them out. Her and Natalie go way back, so she can probably get you a good deal."

"Sounds good," Booker says, leaning his shoulder against the door frame.

Eli leaves. Without that buffer, I take a little extra time putting my tools away, hoping he'll retreat back inside. He doesn't. I've never felt so nervous around a guy before.

"I ran to the store and grabbed you a ham sub," Booker surprises me by saying.

On cue, my stomach growls. "You didn't have to do that," I tell him, closing the distance. "How much do I owe you?"

"Don't even try," he balks as I enter the kitchen. He pulls a sub sandwich out of a brown bag. "I didn't know what you liked. Figured ham was a safe bet."

"Thank you. It's perfect."

I'm a little taken aback by his lunch offering. When he lets down his guard of cocky asshole, he can actually be pretty nice. I know it's only a sandwich, meat between two slices of bread, but it's the thought behind it. There's a boyish charm, hidden beneath an aloof exterior, that peeks out just enough to intrigue me. But, and it's a very big but, it's best not to be intrigued by Booker. He's a gorgeous man, an interesting man, but he'll be gone in a few months.

"I didn't know if you'd be leaving for lunch, or what. Also," he reaches in the bag again to pull something out, "I didn't know what you liked on your sub, so I had them put everything on the side. Lettuce, tomatoes, black olives..." his voice trails off.

"That was very sweet. Thank you."

He shrugs off my thanks and reaches in the fridge for two bottled waters. When he leans over, I see the dark band of his briefs peeking above his jeans. I turn away. Not sure why I find that sexy, but I do. This is all very strange.

After washing and drying my hands, I grab the sub and dress my sandwich with the things I love: lettuce, tomatoes, and pickles.

"Pickles? Really?" he says, pulling another sub out of the bag.

"I take it you don't like pickles?" I move to the small kitchen table, take a seat, and he joins me.

"Nope. Black olives," he says before taking a bite.

"Yuck," I tease.

"How are things coming?"

My sandwich sticks in my throat. I'll admit since the beach, the night I helped him home, the words, *'make me come'* have been on repeat in my mind.

Playing over and over.

"Good," I finally answer. "I should be done soon."

He nods and we eat in silence. How can silence be so loud? I wish there was music playing or something. For whatever reason, I'm trying to chew as quietly as possible. I feel like I sound like a horse. After a few minutes, he speaks. Thank god. "So, I have a favor to ask," he starts.

I finish off my sandwich. "Ok." I already know he's going to ask about the store thanks to Eli.

"I don't have any light fixtures. So I need to head to the next town over to pick up a few."

"Eli thinks you can get me a deal, and I don't know fuck about picking out fixtures."

"Well lucky for you," I wink, "I know all the fucks."

He stops chewing. With anyone else, my remark probably wouldn't seem so lewd, but for some reason, with him, it hangs in the air like a blinking light, a large marquee, announcing sex.

The scrape of his chair across the tile as he rises sounds like a cannon in the suddenly quiet room.

He trashes his paper and I follow suit. "Ready," he asks, grabbing his keys.

I nod, grab my handbag, and we set out in his Mustang. His car is the exact opposite of my safe, dependable mom ride. It's powerful, manly, all black—wild. His scent, clean and woodsy, fills the space. With his height, a good six inches more than me, he takes up a lot of room in the car. It seems much smaller than the last time I was in here.

About a mile down the road, with the tension in the car thick as mud, he speaks.

"What's up with Eli?"

"Excuse me?" His white knuckles are a stark contrast to the black of the steering wheel.

His eyes dart over to me. "You have a thing for him."

I laugh and then realize he's serious. Tristan has had a 'thing' for Eli for as long as I can remember. "No, not at all. We're just friends."

He's silent for a beat, his lips pushing into a thin line. When he does speak, his voice is low and gravelly. "Well, I just figured with all the flirting, you two were into each other."

"Flirting?" This man must know nothing of the sport. "That wasn't flirting."

"Looked like flirting to me."

I twist a little to face him. "How so?"

"Well, the way you giggled."

My brows raise. "Giggled? This is how you think I would flirt?"

"Well I wouldn't know." His eyes flit to me. "How do you flirt? Show me."

I feel so childish next to him. Prudish or something. This man walks around naked and thinks I giggle to flirt. I settle into the soft leather. Part of me wants to meet his challenge, the other part doesn't know how. It's been a very long time since I've flirted. What the hell, might as well. My gaze drops to his mouth, traces the short beard along his jaw, before moving down his Van Halen tshirt clad chest to the bulge in his jeans. I lick my lips and slowly lift my eyes back to meet his, then wink.

"Well," he clears his throat, "I'd say you went right past flirting into let's fuck territory."

"What? No I didn't."

"Yeah, you did."

"Show me how you flirt," I challenge.

He contemplates my request for a second, and then pulls the car to the side of the road.

"You ready for this?" he asks.

"Bring it on." I smile, then freeze when he moves almost into my seat, his hand in my hair.

"First," he lowers his finger down my cheek, "I'd start out with a little touching."

"Uh huh." I realize I'm no longer breathing, and suck in a deep breath.

"Your skin is so soft." He rounds the finger around my jaw, tracing ever so slowly. "Then I'd whisper in your ear, like this." His lips brush the bottom shell of my ear, and I can't move.

Heat rises up my chest, fanning up my neck.

"Ok," I whisper so low, I doubt he even heard me.

"Do you know all the bad things I want to do to you right now?" His breath across my skin is warm and inviting.

I want to turn my head, maybe even kiss him. But, I don't move for fear of breaking the spell.

"What do you want to do?" I ask.

He runs his finger lower, down the column of my throat, and I try to swallow. "First, I'd spread your legs and lick your pussy for a while."

I'm stunned into silence.

He keeps going, "Then, I'd feel you for hours. Make you scream my name." His finger ventures lower, and the three words from the other night haunt me, *make me come.*

And right now, I want to make him come. More than ever.

His finger is at the top of my breasts, and he outlines the neckline of my shirt.

"Would you want that? Would you want me making you scream all night long?"

Before I can say *yes, yes, yes*, he sits back, adjusting himself, and stares at me. "That's a little preview of how I flirt."

I clear my throat, willing my body to return to normal. My heart races as I smile. "You definitely went past the flirting territory and into the let's fuck territory," I say.

"It's what I do." He pulls the car back out onto the road as I sit there trying to formulate a response.

But, 'oh' is all I say.

"Let me ask you a question, for my work. Strictly professional. I'm writing an article on feelings. So how does it make you feel when someone flirts with you?"

"What exactly do you do for work?"

"I run a website. I write articles giving men and women love advice."

I raise a brow. "Really? You?"

"Yes, me." He narrows his eyes. "Why do you say it like that?"

I shift against the leather of the seat. "Well, you just don't seem very romantic."

"What's romance got to do with love?"

I laugh. "You just made my point."

He smiles. "I'll have you know, I'm very good at what I do."

"Sure, I can picture your site now," I hold out my hands, "to get a girl to sleep with you, just walk around naked."

He smirks. "You're onto me. But, it hasn't worked with you."

Although I'm making light of his expertise, there is no doubt he knows what he's doing. I've never blushed so much in my life. "Well, I'm different."

He gives a nod to my handbag. "Pull out your phone."

"Why?" I ask.

"Just do it."

I do as he says. "Now what?"

"Search for Heartbreaker dot com."

I pull up the site and scan through a few of the graphics of couples. "This is your site?"

"Yeah."

I click the latest article to read.

Feelings
-by the Heartbreaker

Yep, you try your hardest to push the horrid feelings aside. Whether it's resentment, disappointment, or worse—love.

You try your whole life to calm the storm raging in your chest. You try your whole life to pretend nothing resides there.

Sometimes, you even trick yourself into believing you're not a hollow shell of nothingness. Until, one day, it all changes. Everything you thought you knew morphs into a feeling you can't describe.

What do you do?
Do you explore it?
Do you try harder to push it away?
Do you run?

What the fuck do you do now that you can't escape from these thoughts you have?
Every time you try, they force you to take notice.
Forcing their way deeper into your bones. Into your soul.
With every waking thought you fight.
You fight to pretend.
You fight not to feel.
You're a stranger now in your own world. In your own body.
The feelings have taken over.
Forcing you to behave as you never would.
Urging you into an unknown territory.
You scream.
You beg.
You wail for mercy.
You want to be set free from the torturous feelings.
Because you never asked for them.
You never wanted them, but they're there.
And now, you have to accept it.
It's fate.
And you can't do a damn thing about it.
It's something that lets you know you're alive.
You're human.
You have a soul.
You are free.

I stop reading. "Wow, you wrote that?"
He doesn't take his eyes off the road. "Yeah, I did."

"This is amazing." For the first time, I see Booker in a whole new light. His prose captures me. "I never pictured you as a writer. What made you start writing?"

A somber look passes over his face. "My mother used to say I worried too much. As far back as I can remember, I worried. Is the mailman going to walk forever delivering the mail? Do the teachers at school live at school, and if so, where do they sleep?

Everyday new worries would make a nest in a little boy's soul, and it never really went away."

"So the writing helps?"

He smirks a little. "Yeah, the writing helps."

I save the website in my favorites as we pull up to the lighting store in Eureka.

"Thanks for coming with me," he says as we enter the store. "This isn't really my forte."

"Don't mention it. I'm happy to help."

"Hey, Cat," Natalie says from behind the counter.

I wave back, saying a quick hello.

We wander around the store in silence, gazing at different lamps.

"What do you think?" He holds up a gaudy brass fixture, and I shake my head. "I'll keep looking."

It's peaceful in the store, no one here but us. Well, and Natalie, behind the counter, who has not taken her eyes off him. It's not every day a stranger comes to this area, unless you count the tourists. But they're easy to spot—hippies, with their RV's and granola laden backpacks. Booker is different. His GQ physique and mysterious eyes make him much more appealing.

So, like Natalie, I stare. And stare. It was the article.

"What about this?" He holds a pewter sconce up for me to approve.

"No."

His brow furrows. "Are you even looking at these?"

I run a nail across my bottom lip. "Sure I am." I step closer to him and check out the fixture he's picked.

It's nice. Normal. Something a new owner would appreciate. "This is the one."

We bring the fixture up to the counter, and I hang back while he and Natalie see if they have enough in stock. I fight the urge to pull out my phone and check his website for more articles.

"Hey, they have enough." He smiles over his shoulder at me.

I give him an 'ok' symbol with my fingers, and smile. I don't know what's come over me, but everything seems off kilter.

"What's wrong?" he asks after we've loaded all of the fixtures in his trunk.

"With me? Nothing."

He narrows his dark eyes. "Did you not like my website? Think it's cheesy?"

"No. I actually am really impressed with your writing. You're not exactly who I thought you were."

"Ah," he leans against the car and crosses his arms, "I'm full of surprises."

"I guess so."

He opens the car door, and I slip inside. Once he's made his way around the car, and started the engine, he turns to me before pulling away from the curb. "What about you?"

"What about me?"

"Tell me something that would surprise me."

I keep my mouth shut about the things that would really surprise him and smile.

"I don't like rock and donut thiefs."

"Oh yeah?" he asks, with a sexy grin on his face.

"Yeah they deserve punishment." My face blushes after I realize what I've just said.

"Well, feel free to punish me any time."

I swat his knee, playfully. "Will you just drive?"

"Yes, ma'am." And he pulls away.

Chapter Nine

Booker

"What's this?" I ask Catherine as she and a small dark-haired boy, wearing jeans and a Pokemon shirt, walk up the drive.

"I had to bring him. Is that ok?" she asks, leery, holding onto a little red backpack with a stuffed poop emoji hanging off of it. She's very pretty today, as fucking usual, with her long brown hair piled in a messy bun on top of her head. The jeans and plain pink tshirt she's wearing only make her more appealing.

Is this her kid? Austin never mentioned a kid. "He yours?" I ask, quietly.

"Yes."

My head spins.

"No school today?"

She shrugs. "I swear they have more days off than they actually go."

"I'm Cooper," the small boy introduces himself. He smiles a toothless grin at me. "I won't be any trouble."

I smirk. "Come on inside."

They follow me to the kitchen. Cat sets the backpack on the table. "Thanks for understanding."

"This house has good bones," Cooper states, his eyes searching every nook and cranny.

I grin at his choice of words. "That it does." And skeletons in every closet. "Unfortunately, a few are broken," I mumble, checking the thermostat.

Cat steps closer, peering over my shoulder. "Is the heat working? It's supposed to be chilly tonight."

"Yeah, I'll call a guy."

My answer to all things broken in this house.

"My mom and I were looking for rocks earlier," Cooper states, his copper-colored eyes sparkling with pride.

"Ah, makes sense. Do you like rocks like your mom?" I smile, focusing all my attention on him.

"Yes. Did you know some rocks are made of gold and silver?" He steps closer, his face lighting up as he speaks. "They're called ores."

I shake my head. "Had no clue. But, I'll be on the lookout for those."

And just like any kid, he changes the direction of the conversation on a dime.

Cooper smiles wide. "It's my birthday."

"Soon. It's your birthday soon," Cat corrects.

I give him my full attention. "That's cool, little man. How old will you be?"

"Seven."

"I'm having a party. Do you want to come to it? Please say yes." His face is a hopeful ray of sunshine, mixed with worry of my answer.

Cat wears a look of 'Why did you just ask that, and how am I going to get out of this?' She shakes her head. "Cooper, Booker is a very busy man. He won't have time for a party." She ruffles her hand through his hair.

His freckled nose scrunches as his disappointed eyes show acceptance of his mom's answer.

I cross my arms. "I don't mind. I'm sure I can free up my time. I wouldn't want to miss a party." I smile, my eyes meeting Cat's. "Especially if you'll be there."

A flush swells across her cheeks. "I'll get you the details."

I wink to Cooper. "Great, it's all set."

"Can you run out and see if my gloves are under the hemlock tree?" she says to Cooper. When he's sprinting across the yard, she closes the distance between us. "Never make a promise to a kid you don't intend on keeping."

"I'm not that big of an ass." I reach out my hand, holding on to her elbow. "I'll be there."

She gives a quick nod in acceptance of my answer as he races inside.

"Here you go." He hands her a powder blue set of gloves, then walks over to me. "Booker, both our names have double o's. We're special like that."

"Cooper, why don't you leave Booker alone so he can work?"

"I'll be in my office." I jab a thumb over my shoulder in the direction down the hall.

"Ok, I'm going to set him up with some books, and I'll be in the yard," Cat informs me.

I head down the hall to my makeshift office, close the door, and fire up my computer to write an article about the effect of the human eyes. The gateway to the soul.

I read a silly fact once that if someone stares into your eyes for more than twelve seconds they want to have sex with you. Stupid, I'm sure. I've stared into Cat's eyes a lot longer than that.

Her eyes are hard to turn away from.

An hour later a timid knock on the door puts a stop to my obsessive thoughts about Cat.

"Come in."

The door creaks open and Cooper steps inside. Curious eyes gaze at me.

"Can I ask you something?"

"Sure, little guy. Come on in."

He grabs a chair and moves it closer to my desk. On his knees, he leans on his elbows as he holds his tiny face in his hands. "Do you play chess?"

I lean back in my chair. "I do."

"I love chess. I always beat my grandpa."

I crack a wide grin. "Is that so?"

"It is. We should play one day."

"Ok, deal. Are you excited about your party?"

He lowers himself from his perched position and sits in the chair, eyes concentrating on the floor. "Yeah," he whispers.

"You don't sound too excited."

He kicks his jean clad legs back and forth and his eyes meet mine. "Some of the kids at school don't want to come. They call me weirdo."

"Weirdo?" Kids are fucking cruel. "Why?"

He shrugs. "Cause I play with rocks. Maybe because I don't like the same things they like. They all want to play football."

I rub a hand through the scruff on my face. "So that makes you weird?" Shaking my head, I blow out a breath. "Being different isn't weird."

"I say that all the time."

I smile. "Do you now? What else do you say?"

"I say you think my mom is pretty."

It's as if this kid can read my mind. "Yeah? I don't remember saying that."

"Well you should be honest," he says, getting closer, his eyes searching out the truth in mine.

"Well, ok, maybe she is." It's as if this kid is an investigator on a mission to discern between truth and lies.

I try to bring the conversation back to safer waters. "So, what games will you have at your party?"

He ignores me. "Is it true you threw her rock in the ocean?"

I cringe. I'm never going to live this rock down. "Well, technically it wasn't *her* rock."

He runs a finger over his lips, processing my words. "Why did you throw it?"

"I'm not really sure," I say, on the hot seat. I was having a really bad fucking day doesn't seem appropriate to say to a six-year-old in a Pokemon shirt.

"My grandpa says when you're mean to a girl that means you like her."

I yank at the collar of my tee.

Cooper rises and peers at my computer screen. "What are you working on?"

"Just writing an article for my website."

"Heartbreaker? Why do you call yourself that?" Cooper asks.

I smile. "It's just the name of my website."

"Do you break hearts?" His little mind is spinning, I'm sure. His innocence unable to handle what it is I really do.

Our eyes meet as I answer Cooper's question. "No."

"Mom's friend Tristan says mom hasn't had S-E-X in a long time," he informs me, spelling out the word.

I laugh, crossing my arms. "Is that so?" I ask, completely interested in this kid's knowledge on the subject.

"Oh my God, Cooper," Cat exclaims, face as red as fire, appearing in the doorway. "No it isn't," Cat denies. "Ok, Cooper, this conversation is over. It's time for us to go home. Let's let Booker get back to working."

He hops down from his seat and moves toward the door. "Bye, Booker."

"Bye, little man."

Cat avoids my stare and closes the door.

After they leave for the evening, I set off to run through the Redwoods. Seeing Catherine with her son, seeing the way she cared for him, brought back memories of her. Her nurturing ways. Her taking me for long walks on this very same street, holding my little hand in hers.

As my feet hit the dirt trail, I try to stifle the guilt of being here.

I push myself, running faster than I ever have before. Deeper into the woods. Deeper into my thoughts.

My past and present intersect, meeting each other for the first time in this sleepy forest. The sun shines, but nothing can be seen through the canopy of tall trees—so majestic, so massive compared to my small life.

I feel like the needle in the haystack, fighting my way through.

I have to get out of this town, away from the niceness, back to LA where it's easier to hide. And then it hits me, like a million tiny pins straight in my chest, squeezing my vital organ in two. Years of therapy, didn't erase the fear. The fear is still there, burning deep.

I stop in my tracks, leaning over to catch my breath, and stare at the beauty around me. Trees so strong, so virile, they take my breath away.

Night approaches, bringing with it a chill in the air. I resume my run, faster and harder.

I round the corner and see the house come into view. Sweat clings to me as I pant down the hallway into the one working bathroom and into the shower.

After I'm clean, I try to adjust the thermostat.

Fuck.

A night with no heat.

Even the fireplace isn't in working condition.

Before I can plan out my next move, there's a knock on the front door. I flip the porch light on. Cat.

"Miss me?" I ask, leaning against the door frame.

"No, but you said you had no heat. The temperature is supposed to dip into the near freezing arena tonight."

I open the door, inviting her inside.

"I was just on my way to my friend Tristan's house." She holds out a grey beanie and gloves. "I wasn't sure if you had supplies, and my dad left these in my truck."

"You didn't have to bring me anything," I say.

"I know."

"Are those mittens?" I ask.

She hands them over. "No. Believe me, you'll be loving these tonight when you're cold."

"I can think of a few ways to heat up." I lean in closer, testing the waters.

"Oh yeah, and what way is that?"

I run the pad of my finger along my lower lip, wondering if I should take this a step further. "S-E-X," I say, spelling out the word.

"Well, I've never been propositioned like that before." She smiles, throwing my words from the first time we met back at me.

"Why are you always being so nice to me?"

She doesn't answer, doesn't even move, but keeps her eyes leveled on mine.

Does she feel it too? This weird fucking pull between us.

She opens her mouth to speak, and then it falls shut. I should kiss her. All signs are pointing to her luscious lips.

What would a kiss from her be like?

Should I even try?

My heart races as a haze settles over us. A dense fog, like mornings over the Redwoods.

I shouldn't even be thinking about her mouth.

But, I'm weak.

I'm human.

I can't catch my breath quick enough. I close my eyes and see her lips. Pink. Sweet. Full. And fucking amazing.

I turn the lust to anger.

The passion to rage.

This is her fault.

Fuck it.

I reach out and tug her by the wrist. I push her against the wall, pressing my hard body against hers.

"What are you doing to me?" I ask, inches away from that soft mouth of hers.

Her breasts push against my chest. "I...I'm..."

She's at war with her emotions, as am I.

My heart beats so damn fast. With my other hand I trace her cheek, outlining her lush, bottom lip.

All I need is one kiss. One taste of her lips and I can pull away.

I don't want to hurt her. But I will.

I'm no good for her. And she's definitely no good for me.

"You should go," I whisper to her.

Fuck. What is wrong with me?

"I didn't mean to...," her voice trails off.

One kiss. Then I'll set her free.

I slant my lips over hers, taking exactly what I want. Not letting this one kiss get away from me, I nibble on the corners of her lips, and with a moan, she opens her mouth for me.

Our tongues meet, dancing together, sultry and provocative, a slow dance we never want to end. I deepen it, pulling her closer, but knowing better than to ask for what I can never have. Her hand dips under my shirt to glide over my skin. My cock grows, as it always does with one touch from her.

It would be so easy to take her right now. Hoist her up and claim her in one agonizingly slow thrust.

I break the kiss and turn away from her.

"You need to leave."

Without a word, she does.

Chapter Ten

Cat

"What is this thing?" I ask Tristan, holding up a black, oblong toy.

"It's a vibrating butt plug," she answers, looking over at me. "Listen, you need this one." She grabs a hot pink vibrator with some kind of weird rabbit ears coming out of its base from her box of merchandise. "This is for when you're greedy."

I'm definitely greedy. And horny. It's been two hours since the kiss. The soul-searing kiss that made me realize something: I need to get laid. I'm still a little in shock. I haven't been kissed in forever. And never like that. Booker was rough—needy.

One kiss gave me a glimpse into what it would be like with him. The desperation, the groans. God, the groans. The long pulls of need.

"Take both of them," she says, zipping around preparing for her CockadoodledOOO party, "and report back." She sets out white plates of tiny sandwiches on the sleek back end tables in her condo. "It's always good to have testimonials."

"How is business?" I ask, lining up cock ring boxes by the wine area set up on the bar. I'm trying my best to block out what happened with Booker. Being surrounded by sex toys isn't helping.

"This is a gold mine," she tells me. "I'm going tomorrow to look at the space for a store I told you about."

"Oh, wow," I say, crossing to the sofa. "That's so exciting."

In the past six months, Tristan has become the town of Ferndale's sex toy supplier.

"He kissed me," I confess as she places the largest cock I've ever seen on the coffee table.

She freezes. "Who?"

"My client. Booker."

She leans up slowly, her hazel eyes wide. "How did this happen? *When* did this happen?"

I slouch back on the tan leather sofa. "Tonight. Before I came here."

She urges me on with her hand. "Cat, I need details. This is huge." She glances at the large dildo in her hand, "and I don't mean this," and then back at me. "How did it happen?"

I don't even know where to begin. "He's selling the Jennings place," I start, "and I don't know, he threw my rock and next thing I know I'm working for him."

"Continue," she says, back to flitting around, placing various sized dildos and sex toys on the table.

I pick up a strand of anal beads, fingering them as if they are a rosary, counting off my sins. "Well there's not a lot to tell. He's not like anyone I've met before." I look up at her. "It just happened."

"What kind of details are those?" She perches on the arm of the sofa, pointing a glass dildo at me. "It's about time you came out of your self imposed hermiting."

"I'm not hermiting." I pinch the bridge of my nose. "I won't bring anyone into Cooper's life who isn't going to stay."

"You can't be alone forever. That's just lonely." She points to the array of products on the table. "These can't cuddle you after. Or pull your hair and spank your ass."

"He doesn't strike me as the cuddling type."

She rises, wearing a very smug grin. "We'll see," she says, straightening her black dress.

For the next thirty minutes, I help her finish setting up while she questions me about Booker. I wish I had better answers for her, for myself, but I don't. I'm not sure what drove me to take him a hat and gloves. The thought of him being cold and trying to man it out, bothered me. Despite his odd behaviors, there's something undeniably attractive about him. Sometimes, you go your whole life existing, and then you stumble across someone who is either going to make you the happiest person alive or obliterate you. They hold the power to do both. And after that kiss, when he told me to leave, I did, without looking back, because I don't want to be obliterated. And now, I get to see him tomorrow, maybe, at Cooper's party.

When we're all done, I examine the set up and smile. Cocks everywhere, mixed in with her expensive decor. I love her job.

"I'm gonna head out before people get here," I tell her. "I have a lot to do for Cooper's party tomorrow."

"Wait," she calls out, rushing over to the countertop in the kitchen to grab a pink CockadoodledOOO bag. "Take these. They are whisper quiet." She stuffs the vibrating butt plug and pink vibrator from earlier in the bag. "I'll be at little man's party after I look at the space I told you about."

"I can't take those," I say, grabbing my handbag and keys.

She shoves it at me. "Do it. You can thank me later."

Reluctantly, I take it from her and shove it in my handbag. "Thank you."

When I get home, I change into yellow sleep shorts and a white tank before finishing up the bazillion party favor bags for tomorrow. I line them up on the small black dining table and take a sip of wine looking around at my life. Cooper's face, at various ages, smiles back at me from the frames scattered along the bookshelves in the living room. He looks happy. I've done a good job raising him on my own. Maybe. I look around at the cottage, we have nice "things," flatscreen tv on the wall, Xbox, but they're just things.

I pad across the hardwood floors into the kitchen for a refill. Red splashes onto the granite countertop, and a fat tear plops in with it. I'm having a weepy wine moment, all because of a kiss. Am I a bad mom because I keep men at arm's length? I can be everything but a man. There's Google and my dad, and honestly, I haven't met anyone who even made me consider anything—until now. I guzzle down my wine, grab my pink sex bag to hide away in the nightstand with my other lovers, and turn out the lights.

Feeling like a gloomy grey cloud, I pull back the sunny yellow comforter and climb in bed with my laptop. Obviously, because what else do you do when you're having a weepy wine moment, I go straight to the source and cause of my newly awakened lust—Booker's Heartbreaker website.

My heart thumps. There's a new article, posted hours ago, titled *S-E-X*.

S-E-X

Fucking. Carnal. Hard.
Sliding in and out.
Sweating.
Aching.
Moaning.
Biting. Licking. Sucking.
Clinging.
Wet.
S-E-X.
You need it.
You don't just want it, you need it.

"Fuck," I whisper into the stillness, clenching my thighs together, wet with longing from his words. And then, I toss the laptop aside and rustle the pink bag to take out my battery-operated boyfriend and come hard to thoughts of a man with dark eyes and lips of sin.

"Double 'o'," Cooper exclaims.

I nearly drop the 'Cooper Rocks' birthday cake. It was more like a triple *O,* but who's counting. I peek over my shoulder to see Booker crossing the yard like he's striding down a runway in dark jeans and a black dress shirt that clings to him like I imagined myself doing last night. Why does he have to be so magnetic?

"Hey, little guy," his deep voice sounds behind me as I slide the cake on the table set up in my dad's backyard, "happy birthday."

"Wanna climb on the rock wall later?" Cooper asks, pointing to the six-foot-high rental with a slide attached to the opposite side in the corner of the yard.

"Sure," he answers. He turns to me. "Where should I put this?"

He holds out a box with a red ribbon attached to it.

I take the heavy gift from his hands. "You didn't have to bring a gift."

"Cat, not bring a gift to a seven-year old's birthday party? What kind of monster do you think I am?"

A gorgeous one.

"I'll see you later," Cooper calls out, running off to join his friends, leaving me to stand in awkwardness with Booker.

He cracks a smile, checking out the array of sweets on the table.

"Cute," he says, looking at the little boxes of chocolate and caramel drizzled popcorn with tiny shovels, labeled 'rock dig'.

"Thanks," is all I can muster.

There's nothing more awkward than mundane conversation where two people are trying to act as if a game changer didn't happen between them.

And then my father, wearing a 'Caution Multitasking' apron, comes over bearing a platter of burgers for the grill, and things really move into Awkwardville.

"I'm John," he shakes Booker's hand. "You must be Booker. I've heard all about you."

"I hope all good things." Booker winks at me.

My dad doesn't miss the wink. He smiles. "Great things." He's lying. "How are you with a grill?"

"Haven't blown one up yet," Booker says.

My dad laughs and pulls him away.

For the next hour, I play hostess, mingling with the parents, trying to ignore the feel of Booker's eyes on me. Trying to ignore his smile when our eyes meet. I'm not succeeding at all. My lips miss the sensation of his on mine. Every time I look at him, I'm transported back to last night. Pressed against his house with his arm around my waist. His body melding into mine. Is it hot out here?

Finally, Tristan arrives. My savior. She strolls across the backyard, her dark hair gleaming in the sunlight, to where I stand sipping a glass of lemonade, overseeing the party from my spot on the back porch.

"Who's that man in the chair over there?" she asks, cutting her eyes to where Booker sits in a white resin chair, legs outstretched, watching us.

"That's him."

"Well, damn. You didn't tell me he looked like that."

"Yeah," I sigh, "he's very good looking."

She studies me. "You like him," she says, matter of fact.

"No," I shake my head, but disbelief gleams in her eyes, "I don't."

She arches a brow.

"Tell me about the space," I say, changing the subject.

"I know what you're doing," she quips, "but I loooooved it."

She fills me in on the spot she'll rent to open her store and suddenly stops mid-sentence, closing her eyes briefly. "Please say you didn't."

"What?" I ask, completely lost.

She flicks her eyes to the gate, as Eli and Austin emerge into the backyard. They drop their presents off for Cooper on the side table and make their way over.

"I did," unsure of the problem. She's never had an issue with either of them. Before I can investigate, they approach.

"How are you lovely ladies today?" Austin asks with more charm than needed.

"Hungry," Tristan answers, turning to leave. She brushes past them and crosses to the food table.

Eli watches her a second before looking back at me. "Me too. Cool party. Rock on," he says, heading in her direction.

"Thank you for coming," I tell Austin.

"Who's that?" He gives a head nod in the direction of Booker, being dragged to the rock wall by Cooper.

"He's the guy whose house I'm working on. He's new to town," I ramble out.

I try not to let my voice rise on each word. Why am I so nervous? He accepts my answer with a nod, and then he too deserts me in favor of food. I step off the porch and stand alone in a back yard full of laughing kids and smiling adults.

"Cooper looks like he's having a great time," Booker says, sidling up close to me.

"Yeah. You looked like you were having fun on the rock climbing wall as well." I smile.

"Yeah, racing the kids to the top has shown me, I'm not as fast as a seven year old."

I laugh.

"So, that guy over there," he thumbs in the direction of Austin, "you guys dating?"

"No," I rush out. "Not at all. Why would you think that?"

"He seems like a nice guy," he muses. "The kind of guy that would wear matching pajamas on Christmas."

What's he doing? We kissed not twenty four hours ago, and now he's playing matchmaker?

"Yeah, maybe." I shake my head. "Actually no. What are you doing?" I turn my attention away from the kids and focus solely on Booker. His eyes give nothing away.

"I'm not doing anything."

"Yes, you are. It's like you're trying to hook me up." I cross my arms.

His eyes rake over me. "I'm not trying to do anything to you."

I tuck back a flyaway from my hair, rustling in the breeze. I'm not sure why his comment about Austin bothered me so much. All this acting like nothing happened between us is making me cranky. "Fine. Can we just drop it?"

"There's nothing to drop."

"Mom," Cooper runs over, "can I open presents now?"

"Yes," I take his hand, smiling, "let's do it."

Cooper moves over to open his presents, and I block out all the weirdness to watch and snap pictures.

Austin got him a football, and Cooper pretends he loves it as my father hands him Booker's present.

"It's heavy," Cooper says, tearing the wrapping paper from the box. He peers inside and then looks directly at me. "Mom, it's a rock. I think this is the perfect rock."

I move closer, leaning over Cooper's shoulder. And there it is. The rock from the first day I met Booker. Still as pretty and flat as ever.

My rock. My chest does this weird pinch, and I dart my eyes to where Booker rests his tall, lean body up against the back fence, one thumb raking over his lower lip.

"That's great," I say to Cooper.

Booker's eyes never leave mine.

When all the gifts are opened and cake has been served, I excuse myself to get away for a moment. I enter the house, needing to lock myself in the bathroom for a bit and get these emotions under control.

But before I can open the door, Booker's hands wrap around my waist, his strong fingers digging into my sides, his mouth so close to my ear I can feel his breath coming out in small, short pants.

He spins me around. "I can't stop thinking about that kiss. And how bad I want to do it again."

Without another word, I raise up on my toes and kiss him. For a moment, I think he's going to pull away, but then, on a groan, his tongue is in my mouth. He takes and I give. In five seconds, we are a tangle of desire. He walks me back into the bathroom, locks the door, and hoists me onto the countertop. He trails kisses along my neck, nipping and sucking. "Booker," I moan, my head falling back, as he pushes his hard length against my needy pussy. "Fuck, this feels good."

He rocks into me, devouring my mouth. It's heady—hedonistic—the way he kisses me, and I can't get close enough.

He pulls back, his eyes searching mine, his hand cupping my chin. "Watch that pretty little mouth of yours before I fuck it."

Oh damn. I want to spew so many curse words.

I want to ask about the rock, why he retrieved it. I want to ask a million things, but a knock interrupts us.

"Sorry, people are leaving," Tristan says.

"Be right out," I call back to her.

Booker backs away, his eyes hooded with lust, and the moment's lost.

Chapter Eleven

Booker

Fuck, I need to control this want for her. Or whatever is happening. Why can't I? It's the outfit. She looks almost virginal in her white sundress, except for the scarlet cardigan and sexy as fuck shoes with red ribbons attached that lace up her ankles. She's taken MILF to a whole new level. I want to keep kissing her, want to slip my hand under her dress, feel how wet she is, but this isn't what I'm supposed to be doing. When I saw Austin earlier, he asked me how 'project Cat' was going.

I lied. Told him everything was great.

It isn't.

She slides off the counter and adjusts her red sweater with shaky hands.

"I'll just slip out first," she whispers.

"Ok."

She does this little shimmy through the barely opened door so Tristan can't see inside, and I stare at myself in the mirror. What am I doing? She has a kid, and I have, well I have to leave.

When I open the door, Austin leans against the wall. The high from kissing Cat dissipates.

"So, how's it going?" he asks, with a smug look on his face.

I pull him into one of the bedrooms across the hall. "You didn't tell me she had a kid."

"Does it matter?" He crosses his arms.

"Yeah, it kinda fucking does. I can't be an asshole to her now just so you can swoop in and save the day."

He takes a moment to study me. Then, it's like a light bulb goes off inside his head. "Ah, I see what's going on here."

"No, you don't." But, I'm pretty sure he does.

"You like her." A slow grin spreads across his face.

"No, I don't."

"Listen," he checks over his shoulder to be sure no one is overhearing us down the hallway, "you're leaving town soon. Cat lives here. Her family is here. I think it's best if you just stick to the plan and do what I'm paying you to do."

"And if I say no?"

"Why would you?"

I step closer. "Maybe I don't feel right about it anymore."

"My friend who recommended you said you help guys get the girl. Well, I haven't gotten the girl, yet." He wipes a hand down his shirt, smoothing out the wrinkles like he's some prized pony. It irritates me. He irritates me. "Besides, you're leaving. Why don't you just do what you came here for?"

And he's right. I am leaving. I shouldn't be pursuing her.

"Be a jerk, and then you two live happily ever after? Is she even into you?"

He gives a smug smirk, and I want to punch it. "Maybe. What do you care?"

"Fuck you."

I head outside, trying my hardest not to even glance at Cat standing by the gate chatting with a couple of mothers and kids leaving.

I should slip out unnoticed, say fuck it all, but instead, I walk to the opposite side of the yard to the small frame crouched by a makeshift waterfall. "What are you doing here all by yourself?" I ask Cooper.

He shrugs. "None of the other kids really want to play with me, but that's ok."

I crouch down with him. "Why is that ok? It's your party."

He looks up at me with watery eyes. "Because, I'm having fun here."

"How about that chess game before I leave?"

"You sure?" he asks.

"Well, I haven't had a good chess game in a long time. I could use the win."

His eyes light up. "Follow me," he says before running towards the house. He leads me through the spacious kitchen to the living room. I drop down on the tan sofa while Cooper grabs the game from a cabinet in the black oak coffee table.

Ten minutes later, I'm getting my ass kicked by a seven-year-old.

"What are you two doing in here?" Cat questions. "I brought you some cookies before they're all gone." She holds out a paper plate and Cooper grabs something that I'm just going to be honest about—it doesn't look edible.

These so-called cookies resemble rocks. Gray rocks.

"Are we supposed to eat these?" I ask.

Cat smiles. "It's ok," she encourages me, "they're just sugar cookies."

I reach my hand out, then pull it back, still uncertain. "Nah, I'm good."

Cat pushes the plate closer. "Have one," she insists.

I look up at her. "You're sure trying to push your cookie on me."

She pulls the plate back. "I can't believe you just said that."

"Is he talking about S-E-X?" Cooper asks around big bites of his rock cookie.

"No, he isn't." Cat gives me the evil eye before she takes the plate back into the kitchen.

"I think you're in trouble," Cooper says. "She just gave you the look." He moves his Queen into position. "Check."

Son of a bitch. I move another piece, and on Cooper's next turn, he declares checkmate.

I stare at the board. "Well, that was the quickest game of chess I've ever played. I'd like to call a foul. You used your mom to come in here and distract me."

"Sore loser. I never took you for that," he says.

I'm denied a rematch when Cooper is summoned back to the party by a little girl with blonde hair and glasses. Go figure.

I place the chess board back in the box along with all the pieces. Time for me to go.

"That was really nice of you," Cat says when I enter the kitchen.

I shrug. "Yeah, it's his birthday. I let him win."

Her eyes narrow. "Right."

"You don't believe me?"

She steps closer, her perfume wrapping around me, making me dizzy. "No, I've just played with him before."

"Kid's good."

She offers a sexy smile. "He's very good."

I raise a brow. "I'm better."

"I'm sure you're the best." She moves forward on the checkerboard marble floor.

Like the pieces of the game, her in white, me in black, we face each other, building defenses.

The kitchen shrinks in size, and I know I need to get the hell out of here before she puts me in check, and I succumb to the urge to throw her on the kitchen counter.

"I need to get going. Thanks for everything."

I step away from her. The King may be most important, but the Queen is most powerful. I leave before Catherine Wells can finish me off.

A few nights later, I pull up to Cat's two-story cottage. Yeah, apparently, I'm putting my own self into checkmate.

I had to see her. And returning the hat and gloves was all I could really think of to stop by. Sure, it's lame, but I don't care.

"Wow," I murmur when she opens the door wearing a flowy, blue sundress that hugs her full breasts, leaving the top swells exposed. She's stunning, and ...perfect. "I… uh… came to return your hat and gloves."

"Thank you." She takes them from me and smiles. Barely. "Want to come in?"

She opens the door wider, and I step inside. Her home fits her. It has a soft, relaxed feel to it. Pale yellow walls, photos of the ocean, flowers on the table. A candle burns on the coffee table in front of the wide gray couch in the living room. Wild thoughts run through my brain about pushing her over the arm and spanking her rounded ass for turning what was supposed to be no different than a million other jobs into me clutching an excuse in my hands just to see her.

She leads me to the living room, and I inspect a few wood-framed photos lining her mantle.

One, of a woman, with long brown hair much like Catherine's, holding a baby in her arms, catches my attention. "Is that your mom?"

She steps next to me. "Yeah, she left when I was a baby."

I reach my hand up, placing it on the back of her shoulder, and graze my thumb along the soft skin of her neck. "I'm sorry. She sure missed out on getting to know you."

She leans into my touch. "You have magic hands."

And that's my cue to put an end to this. I back away.

Her eyes meet mine and then she surprises me once again. "Want to get out of here? Cooper is staying at a friend's house, and I'm dying to get out."

And obviously, I don't do the right thing. "Say no more."

We hop into my Mustang, and I press the button to put the top down. The sun rests on the horizon, not wanting to disappear just yet. It's a beautiful evening. It's the kind of evening that lulls you into forgetting, lulls you into making mistakes with a beautiful girl wearing temptation on her lips.

I drive her into town, and we grab a few burgers. Over dinner, the conversation with her is easy. I tell her the good things, and she tells me about Tristan's sex store. I learn not only does she like pickles on a burger, she also likes tomatoes. She laughs when I tell her to apologize to her burger. It feels very much like a date.

"Ever been to Fleener Creek Overlook?" she asks when we're back in my car.

"No." She directs me past town, out into a secluded area.

"Turn left here." Her hand lands on my thigh, and I suck in a deep breath. "The overlook isn't far."

I don't know what this place is we're going to, but it sounds like the type of place where I can be completely alone with her. A place I can look out at the town, instead of it looking at me.

Every time I venture out, I get the barrage.

"How's your mother?"

"You're just like your father."

"Your dad was a good man."

I don't want to think about any of that tonight.

I follow her directions and park my car in the high grass off the side of the two lane road.

"Come on," she beckons, opening her door.

I follow her through the brush, up a steep winding trail, and past a thicket of trees. Then I see it.

Up high we stand, overlooking the ocean with the moon hanging just above it.

"This is beautiful," I breathe out.

"Isn't it? Come on." Cat holds out her hand and I take it.

We go a little further up the trail and come to a landing to sit on.

It's just me and her in this little slice of heaven. A perfect spot to breathe in the romance of the tiny town beneath us.

"I love it here," she whispers. "I come here a lot when Cooper is at my dad's."

I lean back on the palms of my hands, my legs outstretched in front of me. "Why?"

"To think about things." She adopts my position and we gaze up at the twinkling stars beginning to make their appearance in the black sky.

"Like what?"

"Things," she says with a shyness I find adorable. "I don't know. If I'm doing a good job raising my son. If he'll have anger issues later, blame me for my choices. If he has enough love." She chews her lip, thinking, then continues, "If I've lost myself trying to be everything. Then I feel guilty for thinking that." She sighs, and fuck. The feelings. I've got the fucking feelings listening to her worries. "I didn't have a mom, so I feel like I'm just copying everyone else." She looks over at me. "I'm not bitter, though. Even if I sound it."

I smile. "You are *so* bitter, but I think Cooper is going to be just fine."

She laughs. "What do you think about when you're all alone?"

I raise a brow.

She picks up a blade of grass and chucks it at me. "Not that."

"Well, you asked."

"Is that all you ever think about?" She tilts her head to the side. "S-E-X," she spells out.

I shake my head with a naughty grin on my face. "Oh, Catherine, you're too sweet."

And she is. She stares at me, as if trying to read something in my face. As if I'm a puzzle to solve. A faint blush stains her cheeks.

And now I want nothing more than to claim her on this little patch of land, underneath the glorious sky, out in the open. "This place is the perfect spot to think. Then I can sit down at my typewriter and bleed."

"Ah, I like that," Cat says, scooting a little closer.

"Hemingway said it."

This earns me a little eye roll from her. "He was a drunk who hated women."

"He didn't hate women," I say, gazing into her eyes.

"Uh, yes he did," she argues.

"No, he was upset with them."

"Upset why?" she asks.

"Because men are a slave to them." And that's exactly how I feel sitting beside Cat right now. Chained. Bound. I feel like one word from her and I will be all over her, begging for a chance to kiss her, touch her, anything.

She ponders my words and then smiles. "Sometimes women are a slave to men as well."

"No," I state.

"Sure, they are."

"Not like us."

"How so?" She turns on her side, propping her elbow in the cool grass, resting her head in her hand.

I run my gaze over her face. So pretty. "We're a slave to sex…"

She cuts in, "Oh my God. Not all men are."

I lean forward. "Yes, all men are. We have a hunger deep inside us that only a woman can satisfy. I'm a slave to women, just like Hemingway says."

"Ah, so you're a player?"

I shake my head. "No, not like that. Actually, it's been a long time. I just mean, well, I just mean, I like them."

She smiles. "You're cute."

I'm not sure how to take her compliment. Shouldn't I be sexy or something? "I don't think I've ever been called cute before."

"No?" She looks very pleased. "Well, I'm happy to be the first. But, what have you been called in the past?"

"Asshole. Jerk. Bastard. Oh, the list continues on and on." I laugh and she laughs with me.

"So, not a good track record with women, huh?"

"Not in the least. But, I keep trying."

The breeze lifts her hair, and she tucks a strand behind her ear. "Well, I'm glad."

Everything about this girl is pure. Her demeanor is playing with my head. I shouldn't be having this much fun. I should be reeling her in, not the other way around. It's like with every word she says, I feel myself on the edge of my seat ready to hear more. I want to know everything about her. This isn't how I operate. This isn't me.

"Most men can control their urges. But, I like to think Hemingway couldn't."

"Is that what you do?" She lies back on the grass staring up at the sky.

"What I do?" I ask, unsure what she means.

"Control it?"

I smile. "Who says I'm controlling anything?"

She turns her head to me. "So you're a wild sex fiend?"

I laugh a little. "Maybe I control it better than most. But, I do like sex." I won't go into how much or how deep I like to play.

I don't want to scare her off. And besides, I'll never get to enjoy her. But, fuck, her innocence is such a turn on.

"Yeah, I guess most people do."

And then I cross the point of no return. "Do you like sex, Catherine?"

"Yes," she whispers.

God, so many ideas run through my mind. I need to steer this conversation back onto safer grounds, build a fortress against her, before I start asking her where, when, and how hard she likes to fuck.

Chapter Twelve

Cat

I wonder what he would do if I reached out and palmed his dick? Cause that's what I want to do. I can't believe I confessed all my insecurities to him. The way he stares at me, laser focused with those thick lashes barely blinking, makes me feel reckless and nervous all at the same time. I want him to kiss me again. And again.

But, he isn't making a move. I'm stretched out in this grass with my breasts nearly spilling out of my dress. I've even inched my dress up a little. Nothing. Nil.

We're here, in this quiet little speck of the world, no one's around, I've cast all my reservations aside, and he's not making the move.

But, his eyes are. God, it's like he can't get enough of me.

I smile, seductively. But, in the end I give up. I'm probably coming off as more scary then sexy.

He plucks at the grass, his eyes roaming over my legs.

Should I make the move? Yes, I should.

But, then he stops me with his words.

"I think about how different my life would have been had I grown up here," he says barely above a whisper.

I sit up. "Why?"

"My whole life changed when I moved to LA."

"I'm sure it was hard on your mother after your dad died. Hard on you."

"You have no idea," he says.

My mouth opens to ask why, wanting to understand him more fully, but he scoots closer, reaching a hand into my hair and brushing back an errant strand.

"You can talk to me," I offer, hoping and wishing more than anything he does.

But, he shuts down a little, his eyes shuttering.

He leans closer. "I don't want to talk right now."

And I accept his answer, trying not to feel let down. Some people take time to open up to others. He's like a game of Jenga, stacked precariously, teetering, and one intrusive question will bring it all crashing down. But, before I can think any harder on the subject, he kisses me. And I feel like I'm free falling off the cliff. Weightless. I press my thighs together as he deepens the kiss with his full, sexy lips. His soft scruff adds to the sensory overload. My fingers slip into his hair, pulling and tugging.

He groans, and then I'm straddling his lap.

Our frantic lips try to stay connected as he thrusts himself against me, palming my ass underneath my dress. He grinds my body against his hardness again and again, and I moan.

"Do you feel how bad I want you?"

"Yes," I moan out.

His hands plunge into my hair, his mouth placing kisses down the column of my throat, and across my collar bone as I circle my clit against him.

"I bet you're soaked for me," he says, all desperate and needy, turning me on even more.

"I am. I am."

He runs a hand down the base of my throat and palms one of my breasts. "God, your tits are so fucking perfect." He squeezes my nipple and lowers his mouth to bite through my dress.

Thank heavens I didn't wear a bra, because when he lowers my strap, exposing me, his mouth goes right to my nipple.

And, ah, I can't take the sensations. He sucks the other nipple into his mouth, nibbling and tasting. Every touch of his lips causes a new spark of something deep within.

I want this man.

No sense in hiding the truth anymore. I want him.

And judging by the steel of his dick, he wants me just as bad.

I lean my head back, eyes closed, and moan—long and hard. Feeling. Processing. Getting turned on by every touch.

He presses me tighter against him, and I push into his hard length.

"Keep grinding your pussy on me. Feel how bad I want you." His husky voice hits me straight in my pussy; it's hot.

His dirty mouth is even hotter.

I pick up my pace, with the help of Booker's strong hands keeping me in rhythm, and my orgasm rushes up on me. I slide faster, back and forth, on him.

"That's right. Come on me."

Our lips meet again. This is the kiss that changes everything. A kiss with him as my orgasm strikes. The wind against my skin, his tongue tracing mine, and his hands guiding me into one of the strongest orgasms of my life. No penetration, and yet this orgasm is so intense.

It's never been like this, and my mind races forward to the thought of actually having him inside me. And now I'm determined, more than ever, to have sex with him. Lots of sex.

Once I've calmed from my recent high, and the tremors subside, I give him a tentative smile.

He doesn't let go, holding me tight as he presses a few kisses against my neck. "You're so fucking hot when you come."

I blush at his words and slide off his lap to fix my dress.

He gazes up at the stars, with eyes that are still hooded with lust, and then out to the ocean. His chest rises and falls. I want to return the favor for the orgasm he gave me, so I reach over, placing my hand on the bulge in his jeans, and stroke up and down.

His eyes meet mine. "You don't have to do this," his deep voice husks out.

"I want to."

He drops his head back, his eyes closing, as he blows out a long breath. "Oh, fuck."

I undo his jeans, freeing his dick from the confines of his black boxers, and scoot closer. It's more impressive fully hard. Thick. Almost intimidating. But, I grab hold and lower my head to swipe my tongue across the tip and lick up the bead of precum there. He moans. Starting from the base, I drag my tongue along the shaft, and circle the tip. And then I open my mouth, and take him as deep as I can.

His fingers twist into my hair. "That's right. Suck it."

And that's what I do. His groans grow louder.

I keep sucking, cupping his balls in my hand, as he thrusts into my mouth, fucking it.

I'm wet and aching, watching his face.

"Your mouth feels so good," he pants.

I keep sucking. Enjoying everything about him. His hands twist in my hair, guiding me up and down his dick.

"Fuck, I'm about to come."

His body shudders and trembles as he strings together a few curse words, erupting into my mouth.

I swallow it down as he moans through his orgasm. It is unequivocally the sexiest thing I have ever seen.

When his body calms, he puts himself away, and the look of pure satisfaction written all over his face brings pleasure to me.

He leans over, runs his hand in my hair, and kisses me, deep and lingering.

He sits back, his eyes on the ocean once more and grabs my hand. His thumb traces little circles on my palm.

"I like being here with you," he says.

"I like it too," I admit.

For the next few minutes, we're both silent, listening to the crash of the waves along the shore. My thoughts and emotions are all over the place, and even though I still want him, I decide it's time to go.

"We should get going," I say, rising, and straightening my dress. "Busy day tomorrow. Need to get everything done so you can sell the place."

Booker doesn't reply. He doesn't need to. His lack of enthusiasm is emanating from him like some sort of cosmic force. And it's like someone flipped the switch, and we're both back to reality.

Back to the real world where Booker leaves in the end.

Booker stands, takes one last glimpse of the ocean, before we walk back to his car.

The ride home is a silent one, except the radio, playing every love song imaginable. When Ed Sheeran's *Perfect* comes on, he reaches out and shuts it off. I sneak a peek at him. The street lights illuminate his face but reveal nothing.

Maybe his thoughts are the same as mine.

Sure, there's an attraction, but then what? He parks on the street, in front of my home, and walks me up the path to my front door—unhurried—like he wants to stall the moment.

On the porch, cupping my cheek in his hand, his lips mere inches from mine, he rushes out in a breathy whisper, "I don't know what our future is. But, please invite me in."

Chapter Thirteen

Booker

Everything about everything is so wrong. I shouldn't be here. I shouldn't be touching her. But, every thought I have flies out the window when she shuts the door and drops her dress to the floor.

The perfect tits I saw on the beach are exposed for me again, and I suck in a deep breath. Blue lace panties rest low on her hips, and my mouth waters.

"Fuck," I say, stepping closer, my heart hammering in my chest.

Her eyes are so trusting. So beautiful. And they pierce right through me.

A timid smile lifts her lips.

Tiny demons claw back into my mind, and my neck grows hot with confusion.

Unwanted thoughts close in on me. Austin. My job. Leaving once the house sells.

I take a step back, shaking my head, willing my body to calm down.

"What's wrong?" she whispers, covering her breasts from my view with her hands.

Shame and confusion rifle through me. "I...I can't do this."

I don't wait for her response, too afraid to see the hurt in her eyes.

I stalk out of the house, fire up my car, and race home.

Back at the confines of my place, I stare at the walls tainted with lies. No amount of paint will cover the lies. They bleed through. They rise from the new floors. They will live on even after this house is sold and a new happy family moves in, not knowing it's haunted with fucking lies. I slam my fist into the wall.

Why did I do any of this?

I wish I had never opened that damn email. I should just fucking tell her.

But, still, I will return to LA when this house sells. There's no changing that. There's no pretending I won't leave.

So, why should I get close to her? If only to leave her in the end.

I head up to the attic, not really sure what I'm looking for. I rifle through a few cardboard boxes of things left behind.

A photo album rests between old books, and I pull it out and flip through the first few pages.

Wedding photos of them. Smiling. Happy. Young and in love.

As I continue on, I come across a few from when I was young. A toddler.

They're so happy, holding onto their precious treasure.

I thumb through a few more pages. Me on a bike. Her and I down by the ocean. All three of us together. The perfect family. Lies.

I fling the album across the attic, and it scatters along the floor.

A countless amount of emotions consume me. All wanting their place in my heart.

Why am I even allowing myself to feel this way?

Anger wins out, like it always does, and I head back downstairs.

All of me wants to call Cat right now. Apologize for leaving her. Apologize for everything.

Tomorrow is her last day here. That will be the end of it.

It's better this way.

Right?

The next morning, when I walk into the kitchen, I expect to see Catherine, but instead I see Cooper.

"No school again today?" I ask, making my way over to the coffee pot.

He laughs. "It's Saturday, duh."

"Are you sure?" I pour my coffee, and he laughs louder.

"Yes. What planet have you been living on that you don't know the days of the week?"

"Los Angeles," Cat says, rounding the corner, her eyes never meeting mine.

"Who would move there?" Cooper asks.

"His mother moved him there," Cat answers.

"Yeah," I whisper.

Cat doesn't even acknowledge my presence. "I just have a few things to finish today. Cooper, stay out of Booker's office, ok?"

He slumps in his chair.

"It's fine." I wink at Cooper as Cat walks out the sliding glass door.

I want to go after her, but what would I say? Cooper gathers his books and iPad, and we head back to my office.

As smart and intuitive as Cooper is, he doesn't mention Cat's weird behavior toward me.

She must hate me.

Cooper sets himself up with the things to keep him occupied, and I sink down into the desk chair and open my laptop.

I rummage through my email, and see one from the contractor stating the plans for the house are running behind schedule. So, it'll be that much longer I'll be stuck here.

"Dammit." I slam my laptop shut, and Cooper jerks his head up.

"Sorry," I mutter.

"Only Grandpa is allowed to say those words."

"Is that so?"

"Yeah. Mommy says those words aren't to be used by smart people."

I laugh a little. "Ok. I won't say it anymore."

"What has you so mad, anyways?" He moves from the floor where he was happily coloring in a notebook to the seat next to my desk.

"Work stuff."

"My mom says when something's bothering you, you should go on a walk."

Ah, the innocence of a child. I was that way once upon a time. Everyone starts out innocent. The simplicity of life. It's a shame we lose it somewhere along the way. I can remember the exact moment I lost mine: after he died.

"A walk, huh?" I study Cooper's wise eyes. "Want to go on one with me?"

"Sure." His face lights up as he bounds from the chair.

After he gets Catherine's permission, we set off to walk.

The town isn't a big one, and after a little while, we come across the old historic graveyard.

"Is your dad buried there?" Cooper asks.

"How do you know about him?"

"I heard my grandpa and Poppy talking about it."

We head into the pits of the cemetery. "He's buried here."

The wind rustles the leaves on the trees as we pass by endless tombstones. After searching for a while, we come to a simple headstone.

Michael Jennings.

"I have a hard time remembering him," I whisper, after we stand a while in silence.

"Was he a good dad?" Cooper asks, rocking back on the heels of his feet.

I stare at the headstone. "He played the part well."

"I don't know anything about my dad." He glances down, inspecting his shoes.

"Well, you have your mom. And she's great."

"Yeah, sometimes I wish I had a dad like all the other kids at school," Cooper says.

"I haven't been in this town long, but you're winning in the mother department." He shrugs, toeing the ground with his shoe. "She loves you so much."

"Yeah." His word gets carried by the wind, and I barely hear him.

"Cooper, I wanted to talk to you about something."

"Ok." His innocent eyes meet mine and I take a deep breath.

"You know I'm leaving soon. I have to get back to my life in LA," I tell him.

"It's ok. Everyone comes into your life for a reason."

"Wow, you're really smart, you know that." I smile down on him.

"Yeah, my mom tells me that all the time, but she doesn't count."

I laugh a little. "Why doesn't she count?"

"Well, moms are supposed to love you no matter what," he says, his voice full of certainty.

It's easier to avoid his statement than to put any real thought into it. Yes, a mother is supposed to love her son. Or so they say. Whoever 'they' are.

I change the subject. "So, what do you want to be when you grow up?"

"When I get older, I'm going to travel all over the world studying rocks," he replies, very certain of his future.

"That sounds great."

"Yeah. Mom will have to come with me sometimes."

I grin. "We should start heading back," I suggest.

"Ok." He bends over to pick a dandelion. "I wish you'll come back to visit sometime," he says before blowing and scattering the seeds on the wind. We leave the cemetery, serenaded by a few warbling birds on our way out of the wrought-iron gate.

"You're a really great kid, and I hope you do study rocks all over the world." I take his hand as we cross a street.

"Maybe I can study them in LA."

"Maybe." I smile down on him.

We head down the sidewalk, back toward my house, and I never drop his hand. I like this kid.

Holding his hand makes me miss her. Although I shouldn't. But isn't that how life works—we love the ones who hurt us most.

We walk in silence as my thoughts catch up to me. Why do I still miss her so much?

Chapter Fourteen

Cat

Well it's done. Not sure how I feel about it. The back yard looks amazing, but it doesn't feel amazing. The usual joy and pride I feel is blocked by sheer embarrassment. He walked out. I was ready to give it up, and technically, it's been so long, it's practically like giving him my virginity, and he *left*. I did not want to come here today and face him after his rejection. What kind of game is he playing? Did he think he was making a mistake?

That's all my boggled mind can come up with. He wanted me. After my dress came off, the intensity charging through the air when his eyes landed on me was enough to set the place on fire. I mean, I sucked his dick, even swallowed—he wanted me.

I want more than anything to ask him why he ran out of my house faster than the speed of light, but I can't bring myself to do it. Maybe I fear his answer too much. Sometimes it's best not to know.

I snatch up the rest of my tools and load my truck. Down the sidewalk, Cooper and Booker come into view, ambling their way toward the house. They've become quite the friends, and that thought alone worries me more than my own issue with Booker. He's leaving soon. I'll have to explain to Cooper to not get too attached. Maybe I should tell myself that too.

"Hey," Booker says as they walk up to me. "All done?"

"I am," I reply, going into professional mode. "We can do a quick walk through before I go."

He rakes his teeth over the bottom lip I bit last night. "Okay, sure. I've got a contractor stopping by in a little while about the final repairs."

Ugh, final. I don't like that word; it's so final.

"Grab your things," I tell Cooper. "Grandpa's going to take you out on the boat today."

"Cool," he says, running inside.

"Let's do it," I say to Booker, turning to walk toward the back of the house, internally cringing at my choice of words.

Obviously, we're never going to do it.

Once we're in the back, he stands appraising the bright flowers, new lighting, and new patio. Close to the edge of the yard, the potential new owners now have a special area, shaded by the hemlock tree, with built in seating to enjoy the view.

"Looks great," he says.

I smile, but it takes a lot of effort. "I'll just email you an invoice." I hold out my hand. "It was great working with you."

He flicks his eyes to my hand, then back to me. "Really? A handshake?"

"Well, um, I wasn't offering a handjob."

Unphased by my surliness, he takes my hand. I give a firm shake. "That's a strong grip you have there," he says, not releasing my hand. "Listen, I'm really sorry I left last night."

Call me a coward, but I can't bring myself to ask why. "Well, it was for the best," I lie.

"Ready to go," Cooper calls out, putting an end to whatever Booker was going to say.

I free my hand. It instantly feels lonely without his warm one encasing it.

"Tell Booker bye," I say, hurrying Cooper along. If I stand here any longer with Booker's eyes searing through me, I just might convince myself he feels something too. Which is preposterous, considering.

Booker says his goodbyes just as the contractor shows up, awarding me a quick escape. It's awkward, and I give him a quick wave and beeline to my truck.

On the drive to the marina, Cooper fills me in on their walk. And even though I don't really want to, I give him the talk.

"Cooper, he'll be leaving soon," I say, gently. "So, don't get too attached."

I glance over at Cooper's face. His honest brown eyes shine in the fading sun. "I know. But, we're best friends."

I wipe my brow with the back of my arm. "Well, sometimes friends leave."

He smiles. "Mom, it'll be ok. I can handle it."

I give a little laugh. "You sure?"

"Positive."

I'm not so sure, but who knows, maybe he will be able to handle Booker leaving more than me. Maybe it's me who's getting too attached.

After dropping him off with my dad and being convinced into a sleepover, I drive over to the little strip mall on the outskirts of town to see Tristan's new store. She was so in love, she signed the lease the next day. No thinking and analyzing for weeks with her. She's the carefree one in our relationship. I'm more… boring. When I try carefree, men run, apparently.

I knock on the glass storefront. Tristan appears from the back, wearing black yoga pants and a white t-shirt, and walk-runs in excitement across the tile floor to let me in.

"What do you think?" she practically squeals when I step inside.

I survey the large empty space and try to envision it filled with colorful penises. "It's perfect," I tell her.

"I was thinking I would have a display case here," she points to the left side, "with dildos and what not. And over here," she points to the right side, "sexy lingerie, CockadoodledOOO panties, etcetera." She walks to the back. "This will be the checkout and accessories: lube, cock rings, nipple clamps."

"They'll love it," I say, remembering Booker clamping down on my nipples with his teeth.

She crosses her arms, narrowing her eyes at me. "What's wrong? You look a little droopy."

I laugh. "Nothing. I'm excited for you."

"Is it the kiss guy?"

I sigh. That's the real disadvantage to a best friend, they are psychic. "Well," I can't even look her in the eye, "we did some things."

"Catherine," she nearly shouts, "why are you withholding this type of info?"

"It was last night," I close my eyes briefly, "and it ended badly. And now the job is done."

"Badly how?"

"He left before sex took place."

Her eyes widen and she closes the distance, placing her hands on my shoulders. "You almost had sex. I'm so proud of you."

"Yeah, well, didn't happen."

She drops her hands. "Why did he leave?"

I shrug. "I don't know. Cause he's just here to sell a house and not get tied down to a single mother who clearly doesn't learn her lesson?"

"Oh my god," she says. "is that what you think? Okay," she says, moving in to distract Catherine from self doubt mode, "we're going to have a few drinks and forget all about men tonight." She walks over and grabs her purse and keys from the corner. "Girl time."

For once, I don't make excuses to stay home. I'm all about forgetting.

So much for forgetting. After leaving Tristan, I rushed home and took a shower, even put a little makeup on. Curled my hair into soft waves. These are things I don't normally do, because even if I wanted to, why? I felt pretty sexy when I left the house in my best fitting jeans, off the shoulder lavender top, and strappy heels.

I was ready for girl time.

Except, girl time was foiled, because Eli and Austin were at Old Miller's Pub. And, of course, they joined us. And now, solidifying there will be no forgetting, is Booker standing by our table, looking more unforgettable than ever, in soft jeans and a black Pink Floyd shirt.

"Can I join you?" he asks, not waiting for a yes and sliding into the seat beside me.

Austin signals the waitress for another round.

"Austin and Eli, this is Booker," I introduce them.

"I think we all met at Cooper's birthday party," Austin says, reaching a hand across me to shake Booker's.

After the beers have arrived, I take a substantial guzzle of my Hop Venom Double IPA, very conscious of Booker's thigh brushing against mine.

He takes a pull of his Guinness and sets it back on the wood table. "How's that beer, any good?"

I scoot my pilsner closer to his hand. "Try it."

He lifts the amber filled glass and takes a drink. If drinking can be sensual, this is. Especially, the slow swipe of his tongue across his full lips. And I can't stare at anything else.

"It's good."

A slow song starts as he sets the glass down.

He glances over his shoulder at the small dance floor. "Wanna dance?"

This is a fork in the road. One path, rife with brambles and uncertainty, has no clear destination. The other, neatly trimmed and safe, leads me right back to where I've always been. Obviously, I pick the one that requires the most work, because, well, I do love Pink Floyd. Against my better judgement, I let him take my hand and lead me to the dance floor. He pulls me close against his solid chest, and the rest of the world fades away.

It's just me and him. His warm touch holding me close. Closer than we should be, but not close enough. Until I met this man, I never realized what true attraction felt like. His soft breath grazes over my ear and down my neck, causing shivers to course straight through me. His lips are so close.

"You feel so good in my arms," he whispers, trailing his hand down my back. His fingers slip inside the waistband of my jeans.

And I hope this moment with him never ends. I can't bear the thought. But it does end, and we both return to the table.

"Wow, you two are hot together," Tristan whispers, leaning close to me. "I felt like I was watching porn."

"I'm going to get another beer," Booker says. "Need anything?"

I shake my head no. Just a reality check. "I'll go with you." Austin says, standing.

"Where's Eli?" I ask Tristan when they are gone. She flicks her eyes to a dark corner of the bar where Eli stands with a leggy blonde.

"He's an idiot," I say.

"Who? Eli? Yeah, well, I guess." She takes a sip of her beer and watches them a bit more.

"He is, Tristan," I stress. "Maybe you should move on." Like me.

She shrugs, setting her beer down. "Listen, I have a new business and so do you," she says. "Let's be happy and forget about men. They kind of suck."

"Yeah." I lift my beer, my eyes roaming to the bar where Austin and Booker stand engrossed in conversation.

Her eyes follow mine over to the two men at the bar. She turns to me. "Cat, you deserve the best. Don't get too hung up on a man who's leaving soon."

"I know. I just wasn't expecting to feel this way." I circle my finger around my glass. "Or am I just horny?"

"Listen, I am not one to give advice," her eyes flit once more to Eli, "because clearly I have issues, but that's what friends are for, to encourage you to do what they can't do themselves." She points her finger at me. "You need to be my example."

I laugh.

"What's so funny?" Austin asks, interrupting us.

"Nothing," Tristan answers. She stands. "I think I need a water." I view Booker at the bar, sitting on a stool as he nurses a beer. Once again pulling me in only to pull away.

Chapter Fifteen

Booker

"You know," Tristan says, slipping onto the stool beside me, "Cat is the kind of girl who shelters herself." I signal the bartender for the check. "She's the type of girl who would move heaven and earth for people she loves." She orders a water with lemon from the bartender. "And she loves her son more than anything."

"Why are you telling me this?" I ask, cutting my eyes to her.

"Because the man she opens her life up to better be damn sure he wants to be there."

I look over at her. "What if he wants to be there but can't?"

"Well wanting and doing is the difference between happiness and heartbreak. So maybe he should let someone be there who can."

I glance over to the table where Cat sits with Austin, smiling. Anger bubbles then boils when he leans in close to whisper in her ear. I toss back the rest of my drink and throw a twenty on the bar. This will never work out. This was supposed to be another job. An easy distraction, help the guy get the girl of his dreams, pocket some cash. How fucking moronic. I wasn't supposed to get involved with her. She needs to see the asshole and not because of Austin; who gives a fuck about him?

I stand and do what's best for everyone involved.

"Hey, you left me," I say from behind her.

She turns around, and I lean closer, pointing a finger in Austin's direction. "You gonna suck his dick too?"

Her eyes widen. "Excuse me?"

"Come on, Cat."

Tears well in her eyes. "I can't believe you."

Good, I think. You shouldn't.

Austin steps up and looks between us.

"What's going on?"

"Nothing," Cat bites out.

"Booker, I think it's about time you left," Austin growls.

"That so?" I step closer, towering over Austin. And now a few more eyes are on the situation.

"Take it outside, boys," the bartender calls out.

Cat steps between us, looking at me. "You need to go."

Austin steps closer. "You should listen to her."

I smirk. "What you're going to swoop in now and be the hero?" He stiffens. "Guess what? I may be the asshole, but you're a fucking dick."

And then, I punch him in the fucking face.

Chapter Sixteen

Cat

Ever felt like everything was moving in Matrix slow motion? That's exactly how I feel. All that's needed are some cool sound effects. Tristan's girly scream doesn't count, and I'm too stunned to make any noise. Austin's head snaps back when Booker's fist connects with his jaw. Chaos ensues and we end up outside.

"Are you okay?" I ask Booker, checking his red and rapidly swelling knuckles. He snatches his hand away.

"Oh, you're worried about him?" Austin sneers. "Hello, I'm the victim over here."

"You're the victim?" Booker says, low and menacing, stepping closer.

"Whoa, whoa, whoa," I intervene, holding out my arms. "Time to go home."

"I'd say Cat is the victim," his jaw clenches, "wouldn't you?"

Tristan eyes me, warily. I have no idea how I factor into this fight, but I'm about to find out. "What do you mean I'm the victim?"

I know Austin is guilty of something by the way he avoids my eyes. Cooper does the same thing when he's guilty. Like the time he drew on the wall with my lipstick.

"Well," he starts, "see, when he first came to town…"

His words get cut off by Booker. "And I quit before anything ever happened."

I hold up a hand. "Wait, what?"

"I hired this guy to break your heart," Austin confesses.

Tristan looks as confused as I am. Her eyes dart between the two men shouting blame at each other, but it all falls on deaf ears. My skin radiates with heat as I stand here, dumbfounded—confused—like someone punched *me* in the face. Break my heart?

"Wait," I say, louder this time, holding up a shaky hand to get their attention.

"Cat, I was never hired to break your heart. Ever," Booker states, his eyes pleading with mine.

"What exactly did you do?" I ask Austin.

Silence fills the dark parking lot. He shrugs, holding his bruising face.

Tristan steps next to me, saying under her breath, "I will knock him the fuck out, just say the word."

"No, that's okay," I tell her, turning to face Booker. "What were you hired to do?"

His face is stone, but his eyes are truthful. "Just be a jerk so Austin could win you back."

Everyone talks all at once, and my brain can't process anything.

I need silence.

I need to think.

I need to believe this is not true.

"How could you?" I finally clip out.

"Cat, you have to believe me," Booker says, reaching his hand out to touch me. I swat it away. "It wasn't like what you think."

"Leave. Please." I stare at his chest, unable to look at his face. Because, if I do, I just might cry. He brushes past me, and there is silence until the angry sound of Booker's squealing tires peel out of the lot.

I glance back at Austin. "Tell me why."

And then, he recounts the email, the meet up with Booker, and his preposterous plan to "win" me back.

I glare at him. "You do realize we had dinner *as friends*?" Anger builds at the game they were playing with my emotions. I was like some chess piece in their game of life. Well, no more.

"I was *never* your girlfriend," I clear up for him. "And what kind of asinine plan was this anyways? Who says I would go to you?"

It's as if I've matured, standing right here—right now. Instead of a fragile leaf, curling against the wind, floating through the air, I'm the tree—strong and powerful. His eyes dart to the ground, over my shoulder, everywhere but to me. He has no defense, except, "Well, I figured you'd want someone who didn't mind the kid."

"He has a name," I hiss. And then, I punch him in the fucking face.

Checkmate, Asshole.

Chapter Seventeen

Booker

I need to get Cat out of my system. The backyard renovation is done, and now I can move on.

Tonight's performance definitely guaranteed there won't be another showing. I'm sure she hates me, and that's just perfect.

A sinking feeling cuts deep in my chest. Like a pain I won't be able to come back from.

It isn't love or anything like that. It's a longing of some type. She's a beautiful, sweet girl, and she deserves someone better than me.

Maybe even Austin. Maybe he apologized after I left.

Maybe they'll live happily ever after.

So, as much as it hurt to see the look of rejection in her eyes, in the long run she'll be glad this ended before there was no turning back.

I head home, taking the long way, and stop by the shore for a quick chat with the Pacific Ocean. *Please tell me I made the right decision.* But, I already know I did.

She's better off.

I need to get back to my real life. But, even that isn't much. Lonely in LA, just like here.

I fire off a text to my friend, Declan, asking him to call me when he has a minute. He won't mind the late-night text since he's in medical school and keeps odd hours.

He doesn't call.

And I head home, my mind in a fog.

How stupid I was to let my shrink convince me to even come here. I could have overseen the sale of the house from LA. Never met Catherine Wells.

Once inside, I debate on grabbing a bottle of liquor, but instead, I opt for the moon lit backyard. It's like a spotlight showcasing all the hard work Cat put into it. Even the moon likes her.

My phone rings, and I glance at the caller ID.

"It's kind of late to be calling. Everything ok?" I ask.

"Just wondering when you're coming home."

"I'll be home soon."

Her sad voice answers back, making me feel even more guilty. "Oh, ok."

A banging sounds at the front door. "Mom, let me call you tomorrow."

"Ok, bye."

Fuck, I don't need this right now.

I end the call and head toward the front door. After checking the peephole, and steeling myself for a firestorm, I open the door for Cat.

Before I can even get the word 'hello' out, she pushes her way inside.

"How dare you," she says, loudly. She pokes my chest with her pink-tipped finger. "You're an asshole."

I slam the door shut behind her, following her further into the house.

Now, these jobs in the past always have some repercussions. Comes with the territory. Normally, I don't get to know the girl well enough to care. To me, it was a fleeting moment in a bar so her ex could rescue her, make up for past transgressions. I just played the part and pocketed the cash. And I never engaged with any type of sexual activity with them. Until Catherine.

Cat was different in so many ways. I thought I could control myself.

"Ok, I'm an asshole. I know this. You didn't need to come all the way over here to tell me that," I say, moving into the kitchen.

"So was all of it part of your plan?"

She stops in the middle of the kitchen, and parks her hands on her hips.

"No." I cross my arms over my chest and try to keep my body in check. She's so sexy. Fuck. With how mad she is, I shouldn't even be thinking about how hot she looks. Fast paced breathing makes her chest rise and fall, and I can't stop staring.

I should turn away.

She's angry, and I'm hard as a rock. How fucked up. That's what she does to me.

"Really?" she breathes out. "Austin told me everything."

"Everything?"

"Yes, he told me he paid you."

"No. I quit."

Her eyes narrow. "What do you mean you quit?"

"Everything. I quit everything."

Her anger falters a bit, a small flutter of understanding in her eyes. "And why did you quit?"

"Because, if he wants you back, he'll have to do it on his own." The words feel like acid coming out of my mouth.

"No matter how mean you are, I'd never turn to him," she says. "You think I'm that desperate?"

I lean in close. "I saw how chummy you two were getting tonight."

I stare at her lips, those lips I've kissed before and want to kiss so many more times. Soft and firm. Lips that were made just for me. But then another thought hits me, someone else enjoying those lips. There's a foreign sensation traveling through my bones. Something I can't identify.

"So, what, you think I would rush off and suck his dick?" She tilts her head. "Are you jealous?"

That's it, that's the feeling wafting through me and driving me mad, but I'd never tell her that.

"No," I scoff, trying my best to control this possessiveness that's come over me. "Jealous of what?"

She moves an inch in my direction. "Of him."

I step back, and the countertop meets me. I lean against it. The thought of anyone's mouth on hers unravels me. "That's ludicrous."

"Is it? So, if Austin and I were together right now, you wouldn't care?"

Fire burns through me. "No." I shrug. I step closer, leaning in. "Is that what you want?"

She shrugs. "What if it is?"

"Is it?"

I hate feeling desperate and needy, and something about this girl makes me feel both. My heart stops, waiting for her answer before it starts back up again to pump the heated blood back through my veins.

She moves closer, her full breasts nearly touching me, her hand lands on my chest and she rubs over my shirt, then clutches the material in her hand. "What if I say yes?"

My mind races and my arousal strengthens. And in a snap second decision, I grab her by the waist, spinning her around so she lies face down on the counter. I press my hard dick against her ass and she moans, pushing back, rubbing against me. "Do you want him to touch you?"

I wait with baited breath for Cat's answer.

"No," she answers. "Never."

Oh thank fuck.

I run my hand down her back, my fingers dancing over her. "Do you want any other man besides me to touch you, Catherine?"

She shakes her head. "No."

I reach her neck, and wrap my fingers around her silky skin. "Do you belong to anyone else?"

"No," she pauses for a beat, "only you."

My cock grows painfully harder. I push against her ass for any semblance of relief. "I don't want any other man touching you."

"Oh, God, Booker," she moans out.

"I was never supposed to get involved. Just help him get the girl back. But you got under my fucking skin." I lean down next to her ear, "I wanted you for myself. Do you still want me, Catherine?" I know the answer already by the way she moves her hips against me. But I need to hear her say it.

"Yes," she whispers.

"I'm not going to be very gentle with you tonight, Cat. I've wanted you for so long." A ruthless brutality falls over me—a viciousness to claim every part of her tonight.

I stand her up and seize her lips in an all-encompassing kiss. It keeps going, neither of us wanting to stop as her body presses against mine, and I grab her ass, driving her up into me.

"Don't run away from me tonight," she whispers in between kisses.

I snatch her up in my arms and head off down the hallway. "I'm not going anywhere, and neither are you," I say as I set her down inside my room.

I yank at her jeans, unbuttoning, unzipping—impatient—and pull them from her long legs. I've thought about nothing but her naked beneath me for so long. I lift her shirt and she raises her arms, allowing me to wrench it off her.

My pulse thuds in my throat, my jaw ticking as my gaze travels over her smokin' hot body.

"Hands on the wall," I direct her.

She turns away from me and places both palms flat on the wall. I stand behind her, trailing my eyes down the slope of her spine to her delectable ass, barely covered by red lace panties. I unclasp her bra, letting it fall to the floor, and fondle her breasts.

"Close your eyes," I instruct, kneeling behind her. "Lean forward, ass out."

She does as I request, and I kneel behind her to rub my nose along the outline of her panties. I can fucking smell her. So ready for me. Her legs tremble, and I yank them a bit further apart.

My heart is out of control. A zealous beat which will not calm until I've taken her. The fury grows—desire, lust, passion—all things I've feared with other women. But, with her I want more, more, more.

I bring her panties down her long, slender legs. She steps out of them, and I glide my hand up the inside of her smooth thigh.

"You're so fucking perfect."

With frenzied movements, I turn her around, spread her legs further with a quick jerk, and take her pussy in my mouth. Sucking along her wetness, I run my tongue across her clit. She lets out a long moan as I plunge a finger deep inside her.

Fuck, she's so tight. I keep sucking, tasting—feeling every part of her. She writhes against my face as every cell inside me comes unhinged. When she whimpers, I lose control of everything. A ripple begins in my chest, moving outward, causing a shockwave of hunger to rip through me. A hunger that can only be satisfied by her.

She pants my name. I push my tongue deeper into her pussy as she clenches around it. I need to feel her come; I can't take it anymore.

I stand with a jolt and we fall to the bed. She lands on her back as I mount her, gazing down at her full tits.

"God, you're gorgeous." I lick my lips.

She smiles, and her fingers find the hem of my shirt to lift it off. I help her, and fuck, I'm so turned on.

She lights my skin on fire with her skilled tongue as it runs along the clenched muscles, dipping into each groove of my chest. The heat between us hangs heavy in the air.

I need this one fix of her. Just once.

This one thrilling dance.

This one erotic moment.

"I need to fuck you."

Her deep blue eyes encase me with their beauty, wild and free. She nods her head, giving me her yes with one single sexy gesture.

That's all I need to remove my jeans and boxers as quick as humanly possible and roll a condom down my cock. There's so many ways I want to fuck her. The basic primal need to get off takes over.

And then she flips over, on all fours, glancing at me over her shoulder. "I want it from behind," she says.

I run the tip of my cock along her pussy, and enter her in one quick thrust.

God. Damn.

The heat. The tightness.

"Booker," she cries out.

I rock up into her. The feel of her pussy gripping me is all I need right now.

Every bit of want and desire pours into each thrust.

I push harder, with a ravenous hunger, and groan out with each pump into her.

She braces her hands on the headboard, and my balls tighten when she pants out, "Spank me."

I slap her ass, then run my finger between the swells. "Has anyone ever touched this ass before?"

"No," she moans.

I wet my middle finger and dip it into the firm hole of her ass, the muscle clamping down around me. "Relax for me."

She calms, and I slide my finger in deeper, filling her up.

My eyes wander down her backside, over her soft skin, and to the sight of me fucking her. Everything this girl does is a complete turn on, making my orgasm that much closer.

"You like this?" I ask, knowing damn well she does by the way she begs for more.

"I'm so close," she says. "Please don't stop."

So, I slam inside her rougher, faster, filling her up.

Bodies colliding. Hearts thumping. God, I need this woman.

I'm lost.

She drives me insane the way she moves along with me.

My fingers dig into her soft skin.

"Fuck, Catherine," I husk out.

There's no stopping us now.

We're soaring, fucking our way into oblivion. Into the deep unknown. My fears and insecurities lessen as primal lust takes over.

"I'm coming," she screams, her body shaking with ecstasy.

I want to tumble with her, down into the sweet abyss. Heart pounding and insides burning with fire, I keep going so I can extinguish the flames.

Fuck.

My body shakes.

My muscles fatigue.

I'm so damn close.

Sweet divinity rushes up on me. Blindsighted, I crash.

All my fears are demolished as my orgasm rips through me.

I'm higher than the clouds now.

This is the closest to heaven I can get without dying. And it's the mini death of deaths.

The euphoric state keeps doubling in pleasure.

I no longer fear death, for I am... immortal. The hunt is over.

Exaltation. Victory.

A light brume fills my brain, the evanescence consuming me.

I lie back, gasping for breath. Homeostasis returns. My body still too sensitive to touch and I lie here, loving the afterglow of my triumph.

Until the high fades.

Until the need for a fix returns. My fears and insecurities take root in the deepest parts of my soul, haunting my every thought.

I'll fight to do this all over again.

I pull her close, kiss her temple, and pray I can do everything with her.

Chapter Eighteen

Cat

Sweet mother of God. My vagina will never be the same. I stare at the ceiling, trying to catch my breath. That was… unbelievable. I can absolutely see how sex that good, that amazing, can cloud your brain and make you believe it's something more.

Thank god he pushes off the bed and heads into the bathroom before I profess my undying devotion to his sex skills.

When he returns, the glare of lust still fills his eyes. He climbs back in bed to lay beside me, snuggling me close.

"Cat?" he whispers in the darkness.

"Yeah," I murmur, fighting the sleep taking over. He has fucked me into a sated comatose state of bliss.

"I want to do more of that." He laughs a little, and I smile.

You bet your ass we will. "Me too."

"Is that why you were always naked?" I ask, my lids falling closed. "To seduce me?"

"No," he answers, laughing a little. "I sleep naked, and I like to have my coffee first thing."

"Okay," I mumble, "just wondering. Because it was working a little."

He kisses my cheek, and I drift off to sleep.

The next morning when I wake up, Booker is gone. A crumpled pillow and wrinkled, white sheet are the only evidence he was there. I grab my clothes from the floor and get dressed to make my walk of shame. Things look so different in the light of day streaming in the window. The night time hides all the reasons why I shouldn't have done this.

I tiptoe down the hallway into the living room where he stands staring out the window to the ocean.

He turns to me. "Good morning," he says.

"I need to go and pick up Cooper."

"Want me to drive you?" he offers.

"And then what?" I brush past him and move into the kitchen to grab my purse with him trailing behind me. "I'm still mad at you."

"At me?" he points to his chest, "What did I do?"

I rummage through my purse in search of my keys. "We don't have time to discuss it again."

He raises a brow. "Well, anytime you'd like to discuss it again, let me know." He gives me a sexy smile, and I roll my eyes.

"I have to go."

I rush out of the house, unsure about everything. Was last night a mistake? I mean, I should've put up a little bit more resistance. But, God help me, I wanted him.

After picking up Cooper, my thoughts are all over the place as I go through the motions of showering and the daily routine. Later in the evening, I watch Cooper play in the yard as I rock on the front porch swing. I don't even feel like calling Tristan, because I know if I do, it makes it more real. More permanent. And permanent is something it will never be. Right now, I just want to remember the way he touched me. The way he felt deep inside me when he came.

How he held me afterward. It won't happen again.

God, I want it to.

But, it can't.

If anything, it could only ever be just sex. S-E-X. My phone buzzes beside me.

Please let me see you again.

I don't answer.

The next few days, I get busy in my routine, dropping Cooper off at school, planting a few bushes for the city of Ferndale's Chamber of Commerce building, anything that keeps me busy so I can clear my head. What he did with Austin bothers me less than what Austin did. As much as I don't understand his job, or why people would need this, it was a job. I was a stranger, and he believed Austin's delusions. I wasn't a stranger to Austin. Still, I'm not ready to let him off so easy just yet. His text remains unanswered, even though I want to more than anything.

Tonight, snuggled in bed, with the rain pelting against the window, I seem to be having a really hard time getting my mind off of him. I sit up and grab my laptop and search his website for articles. After reading the archives and a million love advice questions, I realize it's useless to avoid him any longer. If he's only in town for a little while, well, I want to see him again. Feel him again. Have him touch me again.

I'd almost sell my soul for one more night with him.

I pull out my phone.

> ***Meet me at my house tomorrow.***
> ***11am.***

He answers back with a simple 'ok.'

The next morning, after Cooper is gone to school and I get ready, I'm all nerves. I grab my phone and send a text to Tristan.

> **Me: I did something.**
> **And I'm about to do another thing**.

> **Tristan: What are these things?**

> **Me: Booker, bed, and bliss.**

> **Tristan: CATHERINE. I have a meeting**
> **with the contractor for the store in**
> **five minutes but I will be calling you later.**

I text back that I'll call her tonight and toss the phone in my handbag when a knock sounds. All my worries disappear when I open the door, and the air zaps with an electrical charge, flowing through us both.

He raises his brow, leaning against the pillar on my front porch, and all my plans for today fly out the window. Instead, I want to pull him inside, to my bedroom, and have him undress me.

"Hey," I say, my voice barely above a whisper.

He moves forward, bringing me into him.

"Did you want to discuss why you're mad at me?" He pulls back, his brown eyes searching mine.

I do want to discuss it with him, but I don't want anything to ruin the magic between us right now. Because this feeling I'm having right now, I don't ever want it to end. But, I know it will, so I want to hold on to it, grasp it with all my might for as long as I can.

"Want to see some whales?" I ask. "Every year, about fifteen-thousand gray whales swim South for the winter from December through May. So, we may see them."

He steps back, dropping his arms from around me. "Uh, ok. Not what I was expecting you to say."

I laugh a little as I grab my bag from the side table by the door and lock up. "Well, I've told you I'm different."

"Yes, you are, Catherine Wells," his heated stare sweeps over me, "yes, you are.

When we arrive at the marina, I grab the clipboard from the ORCAstrated building, and find a boat not being used today. After letting my father know I'm taking Booker on a private tour, and making sure he can pick Cooper up from school, we find the *Chelsea.*

"I have to snap a picture of the name," Booker says, pulling out his phone. "My best friend's wife is named Chelsea."

"Oh, ok. Snap away." I untie the thick rope from the dock and throw it on board.

Once we are on the boat, I get everything in order to begin our journey.

"It's kind of sexy watching you so focused," he says, leaning against the side.

"And I'm getting turned on by you watching me." Well, I am.

"I like that." He sits down, and I steer the boat out of the marina and into open waters.

Once we're a ways out, and I let the boat idle, we sit on the observation deck waiting for a glimpse of whales.

It's peaceful out here, the gentle sway of the boat, the warm sun shining on the dark water.

"I miss this," I tell him. "I haven't been out much since I was hired by you."

The weight of how I came to work for him hangs in the air, threatening to sink this carefree day.

He looks over at me. "You have to believe I didn't know you when Austin hired me. I didn't know about Cooper," he takes a breath, the wind whipping through his hair, "and I tried to be impersonal, just do a job, but I just couldn't. You captivated me."

I regard his honest eyes and release the insecurity marring how we met into the vastness surrounding us, letting the wind carry it away. "I believe you." Feeling lighter, I scoot closer to him. "So, tell me about this best friend and his wife."

He leans back, placing an arm around me, explaining how he met his friends and how Jonah is now married to Declan's sister, Chelsea.

"They sound great." I smile. "I don't know what I'd do without Tristan."

"Yeah, they made things easier when I went to LA."

A cloud passes over the sun, shadowing his eyes.

"Because you had just lost your dad?" I ask.

He shifts his body, and my hand falls from his lap. "Yeah, something like that," he says, his voice nearly on the edge of breaking.

"Do you miss him?"

He squares his shoulders, clenching his jaw as his lips press into a thin line. "Not really. I mean, sure sometimes."

"Oh," I say.

"I try to block out my time here in Ferndale." He glances away with a shut-down look on his handsome face.

I want to ask why. I want to ask if he hates it here so much. But, fear deepens at the fact he probably can't wait to rush home to his life in LA.

"You love living in LA?" I ask.

"Sure, my friends and family are there." His eyes light up a fraction.

"Yeah, I could never picture leaving my father." I stare out at the rippling water. "Sometimes I wonder why it was so easy for her to leave us." I nibble my bottom lip. "Maybe that's why I like whales so much."

"What do you mean?"

"Well," I peek over at him, "they're very maternal. They've been known to adopt objects and turn them into surrogate babies." He sits silent, listening. "I was so afraid I wouldn't have that instinct with Cooper. Terrified. And then his father wanted no part of his life," I shake my head, remembering the hell of those first few years.

"You look like there's more to that story," he says.

I hesitate but then, confide in him. "He wanted me to give him up. Said he would ruin me and my father."

Booker's hand stills. "Ruin you how?"

"His family is wealthy. They threatened my father's business. Me." He stiffens. "Well, that just wasn't going to happen. No matter what he threatened, he underestimated my love for my baby." I look over at Booker, his brow furrowed, watching me intently. "You can't understand what it feels like."

"Yeah," he murmurs.

"When it was over, I decided Cooper would never feel that sting of rejection. I would love him so much," my voice breaks a little, "he'd never miss what he never had."

He leans in and kisses me, gently, dropping his forehead to mine. "I'm sorry," he says.

"No, I'm sorry," I say, rising to walk to the edge of the observation deck, "that was all very Eeyore of me."

His light laughter carries on the breeze. "Eeyore?"

"Yeah," I say, lowering my voice and dragging out the words, "poor me."

He grins. "Nice impression."

"Does your mom like LA?" I ask, trying to steer the conversation back to safer ground.

He gives me an uncertain look, one I can't quite read before answering. "Maybe. She died a few months back, and I got the house. Lucky me."

"How did she die?"

"She drowned in the ocean." He stands. "Or at least that's what they told me."

And I feel like the biggest ass on the planet bringing him out here today.

Chapter Nineteen

Booker

I should've kept my fucking mouth shut. I don't like opening up about the people who raised me. It's all in the past. How does she keep getting these things out of me? Now, she looks like I just let the wind out of her sails…deflated.

"I'm really sorry," she says.

"What's that?" I ask, pointing to a gray mass in the distance.

She waves me over. "Whales."

"That's very cool."

I wrap my arms around her, and she leans back against my chest.

"An old legend says, people lost at sea come back to this Earth as a whale and try to reconnect with their human family."

"Really?"

She grazes her hand over my arm with a feather-light touch. "Yes, look at them swimming together."

"Look at that one." I point to a massive whale swimming toward our boat.

"Oh wow, she's coming right for us." She steps out of my embrace, and we both lean over the boat railing to catch a better glimpse.

"She's getting really close. Should we maybe do something?" Not gonna lie, I'm getting a little concerned; this thing is huge.

She laughs. "She won't knock us over or anything. I think she just wants to say hi."

"Hmm." I'm not really convinced. The whale draws near and shoots water through her blowhole. "This is insane."

She places her hand over mine along the railing, exhilaration lighting her eyes. "It's magical, right?"

"As a man, I don't know if I can say it's magical."

She laughs. And if anything is magical, it's the sound of her laugh. People who've drowned at sea become whales in their next life. I like the legend. I like it all with her.

We watch until the whale is out of sight and then I pull her close. Sweeping my lips over hers, I kiss her as my heart slams around inside my chest.

I keep kissing her, feeling the soft push and pull of her tongue. She moans into my mouth, and I swallow it down. Feeling her in my arms, relieves me.

She steps back, her eyes gleaming. "I brought a surprise."

"Oh, yeah?"

"Yes, and I think you'll like it."

I smile along with her smile, and she heads down to retrieve something from her bag. She pulls out...a butt plug?

"Really?" I ask, raising a brow. I think I may love this girl. And my cock grows.

"Yeah, I was thinking…" A faint pink paints her cheeks. "I also brought this." She holds up a little bottle of lube.

"Down below is a break room with a couch," she states, and she's already pulling me in that direction.

I really am in love.

But, not really. How could I be? With a girl I just met. I've only known her a short time.

It can't be love. Not even close.

The boat bobs with the tide as Catherine leads the way to the cabin below.

"I've been thinking about being inside you all day," I growl, moving her closer to the couch.

I sit as she stands before me. "Take off your clothes," I instruct.

"I bet you were a bad boy growing up."

"The worst."

She does a mini strip tease for me, removing first her cami tank top and then her jean shorts. It's what's hidden underneath that really gets my attention. White lace bra and panties. So fucking hot.

I groan as my cock doubles in size.

Her bra slides off with one quick snap in the front, and I'm rewarded with a view of her full tits. She rubs them with both hands, toying with her nipples.

"Oh, fuck. You turn me on so much," I say, palming my dick through my jeans.

She runs her hands down her body, grazing over her hips and to the front of her panties. "Do you like what you see?" she asks with confidence.

"You know I do." I undo my jeans, pull my dick out and give it a hard stroke.

Her eyes widen, and she licks those soft, sweet lips.

She steps closer to me, reaching out her hands to rifle through my hair.

I pull her panties down her long, luscious legs, and she steps out of them. After a quick kiss to her soft skin, I put her across my lap, face down, and smack her ass.

"How wet are you for me?" I ask, rubbing the sting away.

"Very."

And she is. I slide my hand across her pussy and stick my middle finger inside her hot heat. So tight.

"Are you going to, ya know…" She flicks her eyes to the toy. "Cause I want you to."

The fact she's not afraid to tell me what she wants has my cock throbbing. Grabbing the lube, I coat the plug with it.

"Relax, greedy girl," I tell her.

She moans when I push the tip of the toy in. My cock is as hard as it gets when I watch her taking the butt plug inside of her. "How does that feel?" I ask.

"Don't stop," she begs.

Once it's in, I lay her face down on the couch and remove my clothes.

"Hands and knees," I tell her, rolling the condom onto my thick cock.

The sight of Cat on all fours, ready and waiting for me, turns me on more than I thought possible. I run my cock through her wetness and then get a little rough with her, smacking her ass before I thrust inside her sweet pussy.

We both groan out curses as we move together.

The view I've got is the best in the world—Cat bent over, taking all of me inside her.

With the toy inside her, it makes her like a vice, and I can't control the need to be deeper inside her, to have all of her. She meets my thrusts, crying out she's going to come. And she does, hard, when I turn the vibrating butt plug on. Pure elation courses through my veins that I caused her to feel this way. This is all my doing.

And I want to keep doing it. She is the biggest turn on. The way her body reacts to mine. The way she handles my cock.

Her pussy dripping just for me.

I keep fucking her, forgetting about my life. Forgetting about my future. The only thing is the here and now. My present. And Cat is all it. She's the only one I want.

"I don't want anyone ever touching this pussy but me."

"No one," she moans through her orgasm.

"That's right, baby, keep coming for me." Her body writhes beneath me. "God, I love fucking you."

A few stronger thrusts and my body spasms out of control, my orgasm taking center stage.

"I'm going to come," I husk out right before my brain can no longer function.

As I come down, my thoughts take off like wildfire. Me and her.

We clean up and get dressed, and then I pull her to me, drawing her to my chest as we lie on the couch. Our legs tangle together, and everything feels right. It's intimate and not what I'm used to.

I reach my hand behind her neck, pulling her to me until our mouths crash together. When the kiss finally ends, I gaze into her soft eyes. "So, tell me were you a bad girl?"

"What?" She laughs. "No."

"I don't believe you right now."

"I was an angel."

"Yeah, right," I scoff.

She taps my chest lightly with her hand, her fingers whispering along the skin of my bicep.

And then, we both hear the sounds of thunder crash in the distance.

"Oh no," she says, bounding off the couch. She rushes up the stairs onto the deck.

I follow.

When I reach the upper deck, the clouds are an ominous gray and lightning flashes.

"We need to head back to shore before the storm gets too bad," she shouts over her shoulder as she starts the engine.

The wind howls, and I hold on to the rail as she steers the boat back to safer waters.

The storm is still nowhere near us, but the waves swell, and the rain starts. Cat tosses me a life vest, and I snap it around my chest.

"Let me help you get yours on." I step closer to her while she steers the boat. Securing her orange vest around her, I stand behind her as we head away from the bad weather.

I'm powerless to help her. We aren't in any clear danger, but the fact is, we may be if we don't get home soon.

And all I can think about is protecting her. With every cell in my body, I swear to protect and serve her. Which is ridiculous, because we aren't anything to each other. Just

two strangers brought together by circumstances and we'll be torn apart by life.
    By getting back to our own reality.
    Me in LA, her here.

Chapter Twenty

Cat

I feel like this storm is a metaphor for my life right now. What started out as a tiny squall has now turned my life into a violent surge of uncertainty, filled with a wave of want and a windstorm of self-doubt.

Once we're safely on shore, Booker takes me home. At my doorstep, he kisses me, slow and desperate, as if he doesn't want it to end as much as me.

Despite the swell of anxiety in the pit of my stomach, I keep the smile on my face that's there whenever he's near and wish him a goodnight. He bows his head, rushing back out into the rain as he leaves my door stoop.

Part of me wants to call out the words I've said over and over a million times in my head, asking him not to leave me.

But, my mouth remains shut. The words don't come. Because as much as I want to say them, I need to think about Cooper.

Once I'm showered and my temperature has returned to normal, I light a few candles, and then there's a knock on my door.

"How do you always know when I need you the most?" I ask Tristan after opening the door.

She steps into the low-lit house and smiles. "I think when you've known someone as long as we've known each other, you just know." She moves to the couch. "Now, what's wrong?"

I laugh. "I never said anything was wrong."

"Oh come on, I know you better than you know yourself." She kicks off her shoes and takes a seat on the couch.

I tumble down next to her and prop my feet on the coffee table. "Are things moving too fast with Booker?"

She smiles. "I don't know, you tell me."

I tell her about confronting him and give her a few details about the other night and then today on the boat. A very g-rated version. She's not having that, though, asking for all the details, and I tell my best friend everything about all of the confusion I'm feeling.

"Cat," she starts, "what are you going to do when he leaves?"

"I don't know," I whisper. "Why do all the important people leave?"

"They don't," she says, her face morphing into compassion, "but you know he's only here temporarily. Is this just sex? Cause I see the look in your eyes."

"What look?"

"The look that says you have rocketed past like into that gray area that becomes…"

"Don't say it," I place my hand over her mouth, then drop it. "It was just really good sex. That's all."

"If you say so," she says, knowing I don't believe it anymore than she does.

The next morning, I skip my breakfast run and instead throw myself into making blueberry pancakes for Cooper and

I. After Tristan left last night, I still hadn't made up my mind about Booker, and whether I can continue this thing happening between us.

We have an expiration date. It's so obvious.

A knock sounds at the door as I fold blueberries into the batter.

"Mom, Booker's here," Cooper shouts from the front door.

I wipe my hand on my apron and walk out to the living area where he stands, looking extra scrumptious, in jeans and a Boondock Saints tee.

"Hey," I greet him, immediately feeling the now familiar pull.

"You left a few of your tools at my house." He holds up a little bag of my gardening tools in his hand.

"Thank you." I reach for the bag, and everything is so awkward between us, even though he now knows my backside better than I do.

But, Cooper doesn't notice.

"Mom stayed home from work to make pancakes. Want some?"

His dark eyes meet mine for a moment. "Work?"

"Yeah," I answer. "I deliver breakfast on the weekends. DeliciousnessDelivered. That's what I was doing when you stole my donut."

"Ah," he says, a grin breaking out, "and all this time I thought you just really liked donuts."

"Well, obviously," I answer, "but I don't think my butt could handle five boxes."

The look in his eyes morphs from amusement to downright sexual. Heat fans across my body remembering how I begged him to use the plug. "Don't even say it."

He licks his lips.

"You gonna stay?" Cooper asks, looking up from his video game.

He smiles wide, never looking away from me. "Sure, buddy. If it's ok with your mom."

This is the thing with kids: everyone is welcome. So, I smile as Cooper assures him I'm fine with it.

Booker follows me into the kitchen after Cooper returns to his game, oblivious to the undercurrents between Booker and I.

The air sizzles and zaps with an odd unfamiliarity as I grab a yellow mug from the cherry cabinet and pour him a cup of coffee. I've never had anyone over for pancakes with my son before.

So, this is what it feels like to have the domesticated life. In all my years as a single mother, I never guessed it would feel so...cozy. Me pouring batter into a skillet while he leans back against the counter, watching.

A warmth crowds my insides, and I realize how much I want him here.

"I can't stop thinking about you," he says against the shell of my ear.

The pancakes need to be flipped, and I focus on the task at hand, even though chills are racing along my skin. I want to toss the spatula, fling my arms around his neck and kiss him. Instead, I shake out the shiver, and flip the cakes on the stove.

"I can't stop thinking about you too," I finally whisper, admitting the truth, hoping like hell the words don't bite.

He wraps his arms around my waist, and I push out of his hold and peek over my shoulder at him. "Cooper's here."

He holds his hands up, taking a step back, recognition dawning on his face. "I'll be sure to keep my hands to myself."

I laugh a little and his smile really is a perfect thing. So true. And when it reaches his eyes, they sparkle.

"How many do you want?" I point to the batter in the pan.

"Whatever extra you have." He takes a seat on a barstool at the island and lets out a smooth, controlled breath. "Oh, by the way, Poppy put the 'for sale' sign on the house."

And the end has come. It's over before it even began. Which is a good thing, I guess. A knot forms around my heart, squeezing it dry of everything. I fake enthusiasm. "That's great."

My hands shake, and I try not to think about how much I'll miss this man. But, I knew what I was getting into, and I chose to do it anyways. So, I need to pull up my big girl panties, and face the future. Alone.

"Who's ready?" I ask, faking a glimmer of happiness I wish more than anything I really felt, as I head towards the dining room with a plate of pancakes.

After we're all seated around the table, I sit silently and listen to Booker and Cooper joke about rocks and superheroes. Their chatter fills the room, but I can't process any of it.

I push my food around on my plate as the memory of Booker and I yesterday together flows through my mind. And I'm not talking about only the sex. It was all of it—the intimacy, the rush of adrenaline when he held me close, the way he looked at me.

Is this what falling for someone feels like?

When breakfast is over, he helps me clear the table, and we head outside. Cooper runs to play in the yard, and Booker and I take a seat on the front porch swing.

He holds my hand as we rock gently.

"How long do you think it will take to sell?"

He squeezes my hand in his. "I don't know," he answers. "But, I'll be here a little longer, tying up loose ends."

"Well, I hope it sells quickly." I try my hardest to sound upbeat.

"Don't." His eyes meet mine, and I almost want to break down right here and beg him not to go.

But, I'm strong. I'd never ask that of him.

Does he feel it too?

"Booker, it is what it is." I put on a brave front, even if I'm a coward..

Sure, LA isn't a lifetime away. But, I want someone who doesn't fly in on the weekends. And besides, he doesn't ever plan on staying here, and I don't plan on ever moving. So that's that.

Booker stays all day. We play games with Cooper, and I even giggle as they toss a football in the front yard together.

Something is happening to my chest, a warmth spreading through it, reaching out to each limb. I don't know how to make it go away. Or if I even want it to. God, what am I thinking?

Every girl dreams of a love so big it moves mountains. I'm not saying that's what Booker and I have, but the pinch in my heart when I think of him leaving, makes me think it might be around the corner.

Later in the evening, after Cooper has gone to bed, Booker and I move to the couch. We snuggle, cuddle, and I laugh to myself at the conversation Tristan and I had about him cuddling. He's so a cuddler.

I take what I can get from him, greedy to spend our last days alone together, in my bed. I let him touch me in ways I've never been touched before. He moans my name. I moan his.

The end is inevitable, but I feel like this is only the beginning of him and I. So many things to learn and explore about one another. He takes his time kissing, nibbling, and sucking along my body into the wee hours of the morning. When dawn breaks, he holds me as close as he can, our bodies wrapped together as one.

"Where's that dirty mouth now?" I tease as he's about to enter me for the third time tonight.

He explores my eyes, the moment hanging between us, as he whispers, "I'm speechless."

And then he moves inside me—tender, loving, and poetic. It's a moment I won't soon forget and wish like hell I would never have to.

Chapter Twenty-one

Booker

"All you have to do is sign here," Poppy says, pushing a contract across the new granite counter in the kitchen of the house that is no longer mine.

I want nothing more than to ask her about Cat, but I don't.

"Great." I grab the pen and scribble on the dotted line. "How soon before I need to be out?"

I never expected the house to sell so quickly. About two weeks after the sign was staked in the ground, we had an offer. It only took a few days after that to accept and draw up the paperwork. And just like that, it's over.

"Well, I thought you wanted this place sold quickly so you could get back?"

I run a hand down the side of my face, and over the scruff growing there. "Yeah, I just need to pack up a few things."

She takes the contract and puts it into her briefcase. "You have plenty of time for that."

There's a knock at the door, and I give her back her pen. "Thanks, Poppy." I shake her hand, and she follows me to the door.

I take two steps back at who is standing on my front porch. "Declan, what are you doing here, man?"

"I've been sent to check on you." His blonde-brown hair shines in the light of the sun, and he casts a broad smile at me.

I say goodbye to Poppy again and invite Declan in.

"Well, it just sold."

"About fucking time."

"Yeah." I glance around the home, amazed at how far its come. "It's definitely been a project."

He slaps my shoulder. "Now you can come home."

I blow out a breath. Home.

Let me tell you something, I'm happier than fucking clowns, or whatever you measure happiness with, that the house has sold. But, there's a sinking feeling in my chest that aches with each breath I take.

Since the morning I went over to Catherine's and spent the day and night with her, I've barely seen her. It's been a whirlwind of frenzied activity. Showing the house to potential sellers. Her getting a contract to work on a renovation for a few of the local schools. So our time has been limited together.

So, yes I'm happy the house has sold, but I need to see her again. One last time before I go.

I tell Declan everything. About Cat. About Austin. About Cooper. About it all.

And the more I talk, the more concerned Declan looks.

"Fuck, you've fallen for this girl, haven't you?"

"Hold on," I say, placing my hands flat on the counter. "Who says I fell for her?"

"Oh, you're right." He laughs a little, sarcastically. "Cause none of that sounds like falling for someone. So, what are you going to do?"

"There's nothing to do. The house is sold, and I want to get the fuck out of here."

"Yeah, your mom is ready for you to come back." He opens the fridge to grab a bottled water.

"Yeah, I know."

"You ok?" he asks.

"I'm fine." Although, the thought of leaving makes me all clammy and tense.

"You don't look so fine." The worry lines in his forehead deepen.

"I am." I move out of the kitchen, hoping he'll agree to my next request. "Want to go to a festival?"

"A what?" Declan raises a blonde brow.

"It's some Redwood Music Festival. Come on, it'll be fun."

He points a finger straight at me, with eyes like he just figured out the biggest mystery on the planet. "You want to see this Cat, huh?"

I stare over his shoulder, avoiding answering. "Yeah," I finally admit, then my eyes meet his, "I can't leave without seeing her one last time."

"Yeah, that would be a dick move."

"Besides, you just got here. Don't you want to have a little fun?"

"True. Let me get my bag and shower. I had a hell of a flight," he says, walking toward the front door to retrieve his bag out of his rental car. "Plus, I need to meet the girl who has you going to festivals."

Later, Declan and I head down main street with a beer in our hands. The sun's rays barely peek above the horizon, and the street is alight with a million tiny bulbs held together by wire, strung out above the crowd.

People relax as they drink beer in red plastic cups and listen to local artists spouting out jazz and folk music for everyone to enjoy.

"Booker, Booker, come watch me," Cooper yells, racing up to us with a hopeful gleam in his eyes.

"Hey, Coop." I introduce him to Declan.

Cat's hot on his heels, trying her best not to look me in the eyes. But, when she finally catches up with Cooper, she smiles a radiant smile, making me forget all about leaving to LA.

I introduce everyone, and Declan gives me a knowing nod, and says he's going to check out the music.

"So," I say to her, slowly, ever so carefully.

"So," she clips back.

"I'm leaving tomorrow." I rub the back of my neck with one hand.

"Yeah, Poppy told me the house sold."

"Cat, I…" She stops me before I can say more.

"Booker, it's fine. I had a great time getting to know you."

Ouch. Is this all it was for her? A little fun. I glance down at Cooper tugging on Catherine's arm.

"Mom, can Booker watch me play a game?" Cooper asks with pleading eyes.

How can you say no to a face as cute as his?

She nods, and we walk around, watching Cooper play the carnival games along the street.

"He's a bundle of energy tonight. He's going to crash once I get him home," Cat says, shaking her head.

Everything seems off. Like she's making polite conversation to avoid the tension in the air between us. I grab her arm and swing her around to look at me. "I'll be honest, I can't stop thinking about you. And that is all truth. Even if Austin put this all into motion, you're always on my mind."

She blows out an exasperated breath. "Booker, please don't. Why would you tell me that?"

"I could come visit. Maybe spend a week here or there." The desperation in my voice is palpable.

"Don't," she whispers. "Why are you doing this?"

I scrub a hand over my face. "Because you're out of control, Cat. And I think you need a guy like me."

She laughs, and it's cute. "Oh really? I'm out of control. Ha."

"Yes. Very unruly."

She lets out a softer laugh, and it's music to my ears. "You're funny. But it doesn't change the fact that you're leaving."

I let out a deep breath. "Yeah."

Before I can say more an older lady steps closer. "Booker," the black-haired woman says, "I remember when you were a kid. Your father always made sure you won every game."

Cat beams. "Please tell me he was a bad kid, Mrs. Dennis."

The lady purses her lips together. "No, he was always very sweet. I think it was from his mother. She was always sweet too. And she sure could cook."

"Yeah." I run a hand across the back of my neck, the balmy air suffocating me.

I tug at Cat's hand, wanting to leave this conversation before it gets any worse.

But, she doesn't budge, her feet planted firmly, listening to every word the older lady says.

Mrs. Dennis runs a finger over her lips, then smiles. "We were such good friends, Irene and I." She turns her head to face me. "How is she?"

"She died." I walk away before I can listen further, my eyes scanning the crowd. "Cat," I turn back around, "where's Cooper?"

Cat glances around, her eyes growing larger with fear. "Cooper," she calls out.

I take a deep breath, and it's as if something cuts deep in my chest. "Oh, my God." I step away from her, pushing a few people standing too close out of the way. "Cooper?" I scream.

I'm in a bit of a jog as I search for him. Cat's right behind me. "Booker, slow down. He's around here somewhere."

I turn, her small town mentality not registering with me. "Are you kidding me?" I turn back, panic written all over my face.

Where is he? Did he run off like Catherine thinks? Or did something much worse happen?

"Cooper," I scream again.

About two seconds later, Cooper trots up the street, smiling with a cotton candy in his hand. I grab his shoulders. "Don't ever run off again. We thought something terrible had happened." I press him to me, holding on a little harder than I should, and his cotton candy falls to the ground.

"Booker, let go of him. He's ok."

Cooper wears shock all over his little, innocent face.

I stand taller. "Cat, how could you take your eyes off him?"

"What?" She kneels low to hug her son and pick up his cotton candy. She tosses it into a nearby trash. "I'll get you another," she says to him.

A hand on my back makes me jump. "Hey, buddy, everything ok?" Declan asks with a sympathetic smile on his face.

"Cooper ran off. I thought maybe he..." I stop, my breathing harsh and ragged.

Cat holds up a hand to stop me. "What is wrong with you?"

"Me?" I scream. I really need to calm down, but I can't.

"Yes, you."

"Do you know how easily it is for a kid to get kidnapped?"

"Why are you acting this way?" She shakes her head, casting her eyes down to the ground, then back at me. "Well, he didn't get kidnapped."

"Well, I did." And I storm the fuck off.

Chapter Twenty-two

Cat

I blink.

The world's a blur and everything's silent.

I blink again.

Cooper tugs on my hand. "Mom?"

I blink once more, and it all comes crashing back louder and brighter than before.

"Booker," I whisper to his back as he stalks off through the throng of people milling about. My heart starts an unsteady rhythm, echoing through my ears.

Declan offers a sympathetic stare, and I silently ask for answers he doesn't give. My bones chill at the memory of Booker's parting words.

Kidnapped?

How?

"I'll handle this," Declan says, with the bravado of a best friend who cares for him.

"No, please, I want to talk to him. I just need to find my father first." I hold Cooper's hand tighter.

"Ok. He's a good guy. He's been through a lot."

"Ok," I say back. He nods, and I walk Cooper over to my father, who sits listening to a jazz band play on a makeshift stage. "Dad, will you watch Cooper tonight, and get him some cotton candy, please?"

He pulls Cooper onto his knee. "Sure, what's wrong?"

"I need to find Booker," I say, giving Cooper a peck on the cheek. "I'll explain later."

He accepts my answer, without pressing for more, and I rush to my truck and drive up the lost coast, searching for Booker's Mustang. He's not anywhere to be found. I'm not even sure where there's left to look. After trying his house, and the local pub, I don't know where else to go.

The moon is non-existent in the night sky, covered by sleepy clouds looming off the shore, helping conceal him from me. I try one more place and sigh in relief when I pull in and see Booker's Mustang sitting next to the lookout spot. After a quick hike, I see him in the distance. Just a shadow, hiding in the night. My heart collapses at the sight of his slumped shoulders.

"That's my rock, mister," I joke, stepping up behind him to where he sits on the rocks.

He tosses the rock in his hand. It lands a few feet away.

"I can't believe you threw my rock again," I say, tentatively sitting next to him.

He barely offers a chuckle, his eyes cast downward, the soft light of the undercover moon shadowing his face from me.

I don't speak, waiting for him to start, or not.

If we sit here silent all night, I'll be ok with that. I rub his back, letting him know I'm here, feeling his tense muscles ease as my fingers drift over them.

"I'm sorry I scared Cooper," he whispers into the air.

"He's fine." I continue with my hand against the strong muscles under his shirt.

"I'm sorry I yelled at you."

I take a deep breath. "I guess I don't really worry about those kinds of things here." Which is really naive of me, it could happen anywhere. "I should have kept a better eye on him," I whisper.

And I should have. Truth is, you never believe something bad can happen to you. That you'll never be a statistic. That one day you can have your life upended in a split second.

He focuses on the ocean, not speaking for a long while. When he finally does, his voice cracks with the first word. "My mother took her eyes off me only for a moment." I suck in a breath, my heart raging with uneasy trepidation of his story. I slide my hand into his, hoping to give some sense of comfort. He grips mine back. "I was born in LA. My mother took me on a walk."

My insides churn, visualizing the scene. "Go on."

"She only turned her head for a second from my stroller." He gives a bitter laugh. "A fucking second later, I was gone."

"I'm so sorry. Did they find you right away? Is that why your parents moved here, because this town's safer?"

And then, he stops my heart with his next words. "The Jennings aren't my parents. They're the ones who took me." He looks down on me, a world of pain in his eyes.

Chills skate across my skin as the realization of what he's saying sinks in.

"They brought me here. Raised me as their own."

"How did you find out?" I ask, imagining the terror of Cooper being taken from me. Imagining the terror of a boy finding out his life was a lie.

"After Mr. Jennings died, my mother, I mean Irene, went kind of crazy." He lets out a deep breath, then continues, "She was always crazy, apparently."

His secret is too big to process. Too big to fathom. A maelstrom of confusion churns around me. "What happened?"

He shrugs, looks up at the sky, and then back at the ocean. "Not really sure. She took me to LA. Walked right into the police station and turned me over."

"Oh, wow." I am utterly confused at what to say at this point. I want to take the pain from him and carry it as my own. "You must've been terrified."

"Yeah, it was a whirlwind of activity after that. I was told, at almost eleven years old, that the mother I loved was a bad person and reunited with my real family."

"I'm sure your real mother must have been so happy to have you back." I give a hopeful smile that he can't see because his gaze is fixed on the ocean again.

"Sure, of course she was. It was a hard thing to deal with. But, years and years of therapy helped me understand what exactly happened to me."

"I'm so sorry, Booker."

He shrugs again. "I felt so guilty for so many years."

"Why? It wasn't your fault."

"I felt guilty because I missed the woman who raised me. She was my mom." The weight of what he says brings tears to my eyes. "No one seemed to understand that. Every time I got hurt, she was there to kiss it all away. Every time I was scared at night, she would sing me to sleep. I missed her so much, but I felt guilty every time I did."

My heart breaks into a million tiny shards for this man. "It wasn't your fault. You were a child."

"My real mother and I had a hard time. I wish I could say it was all roses and *Leave it to Beaver*, but it wasn't."

"I can't even begin to imagine the repercussions of those lost years," I say, still unable to fully grasp the effects of his nightmare.

"She didn't know me, and I was too confused to let her. We never really connected." He looks over at me. "I was so angry for many years."

I remain quiet as he works through his story.

"I was angry at my real mother. I felt like she never looked hard enough for me, or that she gave up on me."

I wrap an arm around him. "Oh, Booker. A mother could never give up on her son."

"Well, Irene did." His voice is laden with darkness, calamity wrapping around each word, sending a shiver down my spine. "She returned me like a shirt that didn't fit."

"She wasn't a real mother, and it was her own guilt eating her alive every day," I say, leaning my head on his shoulder.

We sit for a while longer, minutes passing as the tide laps at the shore, until he speaks. "I never saw Irene again. When she died, and left me the house, I figured it would be easy to come here and sell it." He shakes his head. "All the memories came rushing back as soon as I stepped foot through the door. It was tough dealing with that," he pauses, and his eyes, full of self incrimination, cut over to me, "and the guilt that I was leaving my real mom again. She needs me."

"I'm so sorry." I cringe. "I'm sure I didn't help matters carrying on about a rock."

He laughs, lightly. "You helped me more than you'll ever know." He scrubs a hand along his jaw. "It sold."

He looks over at me, and I feel the force of it slamming into me. His guilt. Guilt over leaving here and getting back to his life, where his mother is. Selfishly, I don't want him to go. I don't. But, I can't do that to him.

I lean back, gazing into his troubled eyes, and free him from his guilt. "You know, everything goes back to childhood, so I have a hard time saying goodbye," I smile, softly, fighting back the tears, "so let's not say the words."

He leans in and kisses me, and all the emotion between us explodes into a fire of raw understanding.

He breaks the kiss and drops his forehead to mine. "We should get going."

"Cooper is staying the night with my father," I whisper.

He stands and takes my hand, understanding my meaning.

The moment we step foot through my front door, our hearts beating in unison, heat heavy in the air, Booker grabs my waist in a desperate pull.

"Let's pretend like tonight will never end," he whispers along my skin.

We move together to my bedroom, a faint whimper falling from my lips as he makes quick work of his clothing. I sit on the bed, watching and waiting, his delicious body being revealed just for me. Licking my lips, I smile as he draws closer, his muscles on display.

He removes my dress in one quick tug. "I'll never forget how you look at me."

I want this man. Bad.

And even though I know the end is getting closer, like a giant clock ticking away the seconds, I don't want any of those thoughts to ruin tonight for us. I'm too caught up in this moment with him. Too caught up in the magic.

He hovers over me, his lips inches from mine, and I breathe him in, wanting to remember everything. His scent. His touch. His taste. He kisses his way down my neck, then to my collarbone, and down to my chest as he removes my bra. "I'll miss this," he groans out all husky, and all manly.

It turns me on even more, if that's even possible. My legs shake, my insides heating, as I pant his name.

His lips are everywhere—kissing, sucking, licking.

He moves slowly, deliberately, backing away so he can gaze into my eyes, then leans in, brushing his lips against mine as I grind my hips against him.

"Make love to me," I whisper, afraid of his answer.

"There isn't anyone in this world I'd rather make love to than you," he says right before he kisses me again, but this one is fathomless, intense—more passionate. It means something, connecting us both on a deeper level. Our tongues explore one another, tasting and discovering, making me believe for one tiny fraction of a second we belong together.

Chills erupt all over my skin as he breaks the kiss to remove my panties.

He rolls a condom over his dick. Then, poised over my entrance, he pushes in slowly.

My hips thrust up to meet him as he drives in deeper.

"I love this," he moans.

"Me too," I whisper back.

And then he makes love to me. Slow, passionate, and ever so moving.

I cling to him, never wanting to let him go.

Once he's all the way inside, he stills, his eyes locked on mine. "I can't let you go."

I raise a finger to his lips. "It's ok," I say to him, not wanting to fill the night with promises of what may never come.

He rocks into me, a bit faster this time, and I love every minute of it.

A burning begins in my chest, moving outward. I scrape my nails down his back, and he groans his approval.

It's a raw moment, and he lets go. Quick thrusts. Pounding so deeply.

I wrap my legs around him, and dig my heels into his ass, bringing him closer. I can't get him close enough.

But, he's the same. He tugs my hair, kissing my neck just below the ear. He moves and moves as the moon shines through the window, watching us both.

I can almost hear the stars sing, a rhythmic melody only for us. I want everyone to know how I feel about him.

My heart hurts, my head spins with him so deep inside me. If this is falling in love, I hope I never crash to the ground.

"Catherine, I've never needed anybody so much in my life."

And I need him more, but I don't voice it, because I'm afraid if I do I'd follow him anywhere. I'd do anything for him if he asked me to. But, I push the thoughts of never seeing him again out of my mind, and lose myself in feeling. Desire rushes through me.

Love spills into my heart, filling the space with each touch of his hand on my skin. With each kiss of his lips against mine. With each thrust of his body, sinking deeper into me.

This is how man and woman were meant to come together. Tears fill my eyes, and when I look into Booker's, the same thing reflects back at me.

He's as moved as I am.

He's as touched as me.

Does he love me?

I wish for it. I beg the universe for this man to love me.

"Cat, I could worship you forever."

"Don't let this ever end," I whisper, hoping he doesn't hear me.

I know it will though, and I shed another tear as my body builds closer to an orgasm which will be the highlight of my small existence.

This orgasm is the one that changes everything; it's the love maker.

Booker slams into me, slow and rough. If one could ever imagine that. But, it's exactly what I need from him.

He dips his head, taking a pebbled nipple into his mouth. His hands hold my body as he rocks against me.

My nails dig into his skin, a new energy raging through me. It's what dreams are made of.

"I'm coming," I shout as my body trips over an infinite void, never wanting to come back from the threshold of my new glory.

Booker pumps a few more times, and comes along with me as we hold each other tight.

No words are spoken as we both clean up and get ready for bed.

Our time is up. In the end, he holds me tight, a tear spilling down my cheek as we fall asleep.

And in the morning, Booker is gone.

Chapter Twenty-three

Booker

Leaving Cat this morning was the hardest thing I've ever done. The sun splayed over her body like a beacon leading me home. As if she was meant for me.

But, she isn't.

I head home in a daze and spot Declan loading the last of our things into a box.

"You ready to get this show on the road?" he asks, grabbing the box and heading to the trunk of my car.

"Yeah, let me grab the last of my things, and we'll get your car returned."

I hate leaving. A wave of despair rushes up on me, and I can't shake the feeling I'm doing something wrong.

But, it's time to go home.

"Why the glum look?" Declan asks.

"I don't want to leave her." Thoughts of last night stream through my mind like an unwanted slide show I can't turn off.

He shakes his head. "I hate to be an asshole and state the obvious, but she has a kid. You need to think about that. Do you love her? Would you move here and be a stepdad?"

"Well, I can't do that, now can I?" And my head dizzies out of control.

Turbulence shoots through me at the realization of Declan's words. He's right.

What am I doing? I can't move here.

"Give it some time, man."

And I pack up the rest of my things to get out of this small town that has a big hold on me.

After driving to the rental place to return Declan's car, we begin the long journey home. With a quick detour to Catherine's place, I drop a letter into her mailbox.

She isn't home, and more than anything I want to see her one last time.

But, I don't.

"I can't believe I'm leaving here," I say to Declan as I pull onto the interstate.

"Booker, I'm really proud of you. You've handled a lot in your life."

I grip the steering wheel lightly, tapping my thumb against the leather. "Yeah, I need to see my mom."

The 101 becomes a constant reminder of what I'm leaving behind as the lines of the highway blend together.

The lights of LA blind me a little over ten hours later when we finally make it to town.

"I'll drop you at your place," I say.

"You gonna be ok tonight?"

"Sure," I answer, knowing it's a lie.

I take out my phone to stare at it for the millionth time this morning, wondering if I should call Cat. A bunch of different scenarios have been cooked up by me, and I figure I can just call her to see how she's doing. But, I don't.

The past few months have been the longest and shortest of my life. It seemed like forever to get that house into good enough condition to sell, but I didn't get to spend enough time with Cat.

I get dressed and head to my mother's house, right down the street from mine. Our history is built with regret, guilt, and shame. I'm tired of the lies. We never formed that connection, you know, that bond, the one that's so special between a mother and her son. The one Catherine and Cooper share.

I pull up to my mom's brick duplex, park my Mustang, and walk up the cobblestone path.

Catherine would probably love the path lined with daffodils on each side. Or she'd think they're a weed, and hate it...either way, I miss her. Cooper's dad is a fool for giving them up.

But it takes more than having a dick to be a father. Look at my real dad. Eventually, when it sunk in I might not be coming back, the blame started. He left, started a new family. Even when I came back, he never really wanted much to do with me. Sure, I'd talk to him over the years, but nothing substantial.

I'm sure in some fucked up, inner child psychological bs that my shrink is always spewing, I thought those jobs I took was helping them avoid the assholes like my dad and Cooper's.

With heavy footsteps, I walk up the concrete steps, hoping she didn't throw away five years of sobriety in the few months I was gone. I guess we have the Jennings to thank for that too.

I ring the doorbell. A few minutes later the door swings open.

"Booker," she greets me, smiling. She is exactly like me, well sort of. Dark hair, dark eyes, and a smile that can lift anyone's sorrows.

"Hey, Mom." I step inside her house, and after she closes the door, I grab a hold of her, pulling her into my chest, wrapping my arms around her.

She hugs me tighter than she ever has before. "I was so worried about you in Ferndale."

"Being in Ferndale was weird," I start. "Back in that house." I shake my head, no more words coming to mind.

She leads me further into the house, to the living room, and we sit on her gray sofa that replaced the tan one she stumbled and stained with red wine. My eyes sweep the room for any signs she's been drinking. None. She's good at hiding it, though. During my teens, when my rebellion stage kicked in, my mother turned to alcohol. Lived on it. At first, she hid it from me, and then together we hid it from others. Until the day I found her—rock bottom—lying in a puddle of her own vomit. For a moment, I thought she was dead. Almost wished she was. Then, I added that guilt to all the others.

"I'm sorry we never had the life you always wanted," I tell her, saying the words I've never said.

"Booker," her eyes adopt a hint of sadness. "I never expected you not to miss them."

"It's fine," I give her my defense mechanism saying. It falls from my lips whenever I don't want to face what's coming next.

I rise from the couch, heading into her kitchen, to check for any liquor.

I scan the room. Nothing. Tile countertops have no tumblers or wine glasses on them. Everything is neat and tidy. A vase filled with fresh flowers sits on the small island. I'll never be able to look at another flower without thinking of Cat.

"It's not fine," she says, entering the kitchen. She moves to the fridge to take out two bottled waters and sets them on the island. "I've only ever wanted happiness for you."

Happiness. I don't even know what that means anymore. I've spent my whole adult life taking care of my mother, always putting myself second, that I don't know any other way.

"I am happy." I had a taste with Cat, anyways.

She raises a brow. "Booker? Are you though?"

I laugh. "Sure."

"I think you needed that closure." She grabs a dishtowel and runs it over the counter. "Even though I wasn't too happy about it. I accept that you needed it."

"Well, I'm back now, so we can return to normal."

She turns. "And what's normal?"

"Our life."

She sets the towel down and shakes her head. "Booker, I don't need you to take care of me anymore." She takes a deep breath. "It's terrible what happened to you, to me." She pauses. "I know I made some horrible mistakes. I hated those people for taking you away. But, I'm never going back to the drinking. It took a long time to realize alcohol only hides your problems, it doesn't fix them. It's time for you to stop worrying about me." Her eyes run over my face, and she smiles, softly. "You've always been a worrier."

I run both hands through my hair. "It's my job to take care of you."

This is me. And she's mine to protect. I swore to myself, because of what the Jennings put her through, that I would forever take care of her. She deserved better than to have her son ripped from her. Years of her worrying about whether her son was dead or alive, transferred to me in a heartbeat. Now, I take her worry. I take her pain and guilt.

"Look at me." Her eyes fill with tears. "I'm the parent. Not you. We lost a lot of years. Let's not lose anymore. Let go of this guilt; it's not yours."

I let her words sink in. Really sink in.

"I met someone there," I say.

"You did?" she asks, her eyes lighting up.

And then, I finally tell her about Catherine and Cooper.

"I never fully realized what you went through until one night when Cooper went missing."

After she asks if he's ok, and gets the details, she tells me one simple thing, "Kurt says we can't control our destiny, only help it out along the way."

I think about the rock with Cat and smile a little.

"Is that a smile?" she teases.

"Maybe," I answer. "Wait, who's Kurt?"

Her eyes light up like she can't wait to tell me something. "I met someone." She holds a hand up to stop me from interjecting. "His name is Kurt. We've been dating for a few months."

It takes my brain a second to catch up, but I finally comprehend what she's trying to tell me. "God, I leave town and come back and you have a boyfriend." I laugh a little.

For the next few hours we talk about everything. About my childhood, about letting things go, and moving forward.

She tells me all about Kurt. He owns a backpack company, and loves to fish and hike. She seems happy. And for the first time, I let go of some of the guilt.

Later, I examine the pictures of me growing up lining the fireplace mantle: my best friends and I in the woods, football games, a shot of my mother and I at Disneyland.

Even if my mother went through a few bumps in the road, we're headed to a better place now, and I'm happy that she's happy.

As I'm leaving I lean over to hug her once more. "Now, I need to meet this Kurt before things get any more serious." I kiss her cheek.

She shines. "He can't wait to meet you." And then she holds her words in, the words I can tell she's dying to ask. Finally she says, "Do you plan on seeing this Catherine again?"

I shake my head. "She's my past. Keep moving forward, right?" I try to grin but fail.

"You have a big heart, Booker. And you have so much of it to give to someone. Maybe it's her." She fixes her eyes directly on mine. "No matter where you are, you'll always be with me."

I smile, saying nothing more.

Now, if only the sinking feeling in the pit of my chest would subside. My heart hangs heavy with uncertainty, fighting the feeling I don't want to admit I have away.

Chapter Twenty-four

Cat

Dear Catherine,

I wish I could have stayed with you, but life has other plans for us. I won't ever forget you.

There's only a few sights equal to the rose in full bloom, but you Catherine are far better than all the roses in the world.

-Booker

The letter has been read so many times the ink has smeared in spots.

After Booker leaves, I stick to what I know. I work, come home, and spend time with Cooper. It's true I'm not my best self these days, but I'm trying my hardest to reassure myself that it's all for the best.

But, since I'm not entirely sure and still in the poor me stages, every evening, I scour Booker's website. Unsure exactly what I'm searching for, I click and click and read every article he writes. Maybe looking for a clue, anything that will help ease the pain.

One evening, after Cooper is sound asleep, I pull up his site, and read his words:

The Dance

By the Heartbreaker

To one simple song of my life, we danced.
We moved to the beat. Just you and me.
We swayed to the rhythm. Just you and me.
And for one moment we were happy.
Everything fell into place.
Everything was right in the world.
And we no longer feared anything.
I was with you…
You were with me...
You made the endless pain bearable.
I'm a simple writer, but a complicated man, and I've never danced before.
But, with you, it didn't matter.
You had never danced either, and we stumbled through each step...together.
It was perfect.
For one moment, we shared everything.
It was us. us us us.
Dreams, hopes, wishes.
Secrets.
Because it takes everything you've ever wanted, and then losing it, to really know what dancing is.
But, the song ended.
You left the floor, and I'm left alone.
Facing the world as one.
Facing it as me.
And you facing it as you.
I never planned this life.

I never wanted this.
I built the walls to ensure my safety.
But, you broke through it all to find the real me.
You pieced me together again, and now you're gone.
I'll never forget the time with you.
The feel of you.
Your touch. Your kiss.
I'll never forget you. you you you you….
And I hope you never forget me. me me me me me...

A big fat tear drops on my keyboard. I close my eyes, remembering our last night together. I'll never forget him.

I shut my laptop and stare out the window at the breathtaking view of the Redwoods. Lightning flashes, but no rain comes. He left and took with him the rain. The rain needed to keep everything alive.

I head down the hall, open the door to Cooper's room, and pull the *Rockman* comforter up over him. My mind drifts to the night we thought he was missing. The frantic look in Booker's eyes.

Another tear spills from my eye, and I brush it away. I don't know how long I stand here, leaning against the frame of the door, watching.

What if something bad had happened?

A knock at my front door breaks me from my thoughts, and I take one more look at my son before answering the door.

"I felt the universe pulling me here tonight, you ok?" Tristan asks as I open it.

I let her inside, and we both sit on the couch, kicking our feet onto the coffee table.

"I miss him," I admit.

"I miss him for you."

"What do you mean?" I ask. She heads into the kitchen to get a drink, and I follow and find the wine.

"I've never seen you so happy."

After pouring us both a glass, we sit at the island.

I shake my head. "I've always been happy. I don't need a man to make me happy."

She takes a sip of her wine, then smiles. "I know you don't. But, you were different with him."

"Well, it doesn't matter now," I say, staring at the dark red in my glass. "He's back where he belongs...in LA."

"Maybe you should go and see him."

"And say what? 'Let's have a long-distance relationship?' I have Cooper to think about."

She points her glass at me. "Listen, I love that little boy as if he were my own, but sometimes you need to think about your happiness."

"I do." I look over at her. "He's already attached, and what if it ends? I don't want him to be unhappy."

I rise, heading back to the living room wanting to escape how much of what I just said applies to me too.

She drops down beside me on the couch. "If you're happy then Cooper will be too."

I stretch my legs, putting my feet on the coffee table. "And really, he annoyed me more than made me happy."

She smacks my leg. "You know that's not true. That man made you giddy."

I laugh a little. "Maybe."

"I love you, Cat," she gets very serious, serious enough that I want to believe her next words, "and I think he does too."

I stare at my pink toenails. "Yeah, I doubt it. I'm sure he's forgotten all about Ferndale."

And I wouldn't blame him a bit. I tell Tristan the story of Booker's childhood. About what the Jennings did to him, and all his darkness involving Ferndale.

"Wow," she says. "That's unbelievable."

"I think about Cooper," tears blur my vision, "how scared he would be." I drop my head back onto the couch. "He thought those were his parents, you know? He was a just a little boy. A child doesn't understand they're bad people; he just wants his mom back."

She shakes her head. "I can't imagine having my life upended like that."

"There's no way I could ask or expect him to be here, but," another tear trickles out, and I swipe it away, "I miss him so much."

She wraps an arm around me. "I know you do."

After a little while, she heads home, and I am once again left alone with my thoughts. Should I go to LA? And tell him what?

Because what I really want from him, I don't think he's willing to give.

Chapter Twenty-five

Booker

The past week I've had an acid-churning ache in my gut that won't go away.

I'm tense and nervous, and I can't pinpoint exactly what's wrong.

No matter what I do, the feeling's still there. Like a rock weighing down my chest, and I can't fucking breathe. The bags under my eyes are evidence of the sleepless nights I've endured. The nights where I just lie awake and think. And think and think.

The sun shines. The birds chirp. But, neither of those things make me any happier today.

When I met Kurt, my mother asked me about Cat again, asked if I talked to her.

And the truth is, it's all I can think about.

But, fear holds me back.

Fear of what, I'm not too sure. Fear of failing I guess. Or maybe it's fear of rejection.

I've been so worried about everyone my whole life, that I've never taken any risks for myself.

I kick my toes along the sand of the beach. A shiny white rock catches my attention, and I bend over to pick it up.

I spin it around in my hands, and smile when I think of how much Cooper would love this one.

The edginess to it, the smooth surface on one side, the rough on the other. It reminds me of me.

How not everyone is perfect. Nothing in life is perfect. It's one of the hardest things to accept.

You start out in life believing in make-believe and that all things work out. That everyone gets a happy ending, and that just isn't true.

I feel disconnected from my life now. Like I'm watching from the bleachers, unable to cheer myself on.

But, I keep watching, waiting for the moment I can finally join in.

My mother and Kurt are happy, but for some reason, I can't find joy in anything. Like I'm just a soulless life walking among strangers.

Later in the evening, I head to the bar to catch up with my friends.

Jonah and his wife, Chelsea, are there, holding hands. Everyone's so fucking happy. Chelsea's friend, Gidget, sits across from me at the tarnished, wooden table, and Declan grins as he grabs another Yuengling from the waitress. Ethan jokes with Jonah, but my mind is no longer in this loud, chaotic bar. It's back with thoughts of high spring and the slow-paced rhythm of a small town.

I'm back in Ferndale, thinking of Catherine.

The overlook.

The lush greenery.

The kissing.

"What's wrong with you?" Chelsea asks from across the table.

I take a long pull of my beer, enjoying the dense hoppy flavor. "Not much."

"I know what it is." Declan says, pointing his green, glass-bottled beer at me before taking a sip. "It's that sexy little brunette you can't stop thinking about,"

"Oh?" Chelsea's eyes light up. "Did you meet someone?"

"Yes. No. Sort of." I shoot my eyes at Declan. "Shut up. And don't fucking say she's sexy again."

"Just proved my point," Declan smirks.

"Are you in love?" Chelsea asks, not letting it go.

It's such an odd question, but not one I want to put a lot of thought into right now. So, I shake my head. "No, I'm not ready."

Chelsea leans forward. "No one's ever ready to fall in love. It just happens. It consumes you and takes over your world." When she stops to take a deep breath, Jonah leans over and kisses her cheek. "But, I can tell, Booker," she says, full of wisdom, "you're in love."

She can't be serious, can she? Do I look like I'm in love? I roll my eyes, and lean back in my chair. "Oh yeah? You can tell?"

Chelsea smiles conspiratorially to her friend Gidget. "Gidg, when I was all sad about whether I loved Jonah, I had the same expression Booker has, right?"

"Definitely," Chelsea's petite brunette friend says.

"I'm no good for her. She has a kid, and I don't know how to be a dad." I shift in my seat. "Besides, I can't leave my mom, she needs me."

"Are you kidding?" Ethan starts, his green eyes focusing on me. "You're one of the best people I know. There isn't anything you wouldn't do for someone you care about." He leans forward. "And as for your mother, she can take care of herself."

Declan chimes in, "No, he's right. We all stopped by to check on your mom while you were out of town. She's fine, Book."

I take another drink of my beer and lean back in the padded-wood chair. "Maybe."

"Not maybe," Declan says. "It's time for you to live your life."

I run my hand over the stubble along my jawline. "It's risky."

"Everything in life is a little risky," Declan says, eyeing Chelsea's brunette friend before his gaze lands back on me. "And everything worth taking a risk for is usually worth it."

"What if she says no?"

Declan laughs a little before taking another pull of his beer. "I met her. That girl has feelings. She wouldn't say no."

Is he right? I squash the thought. "I can't move to Ferndale."

"Why not?" Chelsea asks. "You work from home. You can live anywhere." She reaches over and places her hand atop mine. "And trust me, your mom would be happy for you."

"You guys trying to get rid of me?" I crack an edgy grin. It isn't much of a defense, but it's effective, because everyone at the table glances to one another.

"Never, dude," Jonah adds, finally speaking up. "But, if you've met someone who makes you happy, what the fuck are you even still doing here?"

"But, what if she says no?" I say, again, setting my beer down.

"What if she says yes?" Jonah says back, testing me.

"Booker, she'd be an idiot not to want you in her life," Chelsea adds, "and you wouldn't love her if she was."

Ok, yes, she's right. I know I'm in love with Catherine Wells. Every bone in my body knows it's true. I have to stop fighting it.

"If you don't at least try, you'll never know," she finishes.

"Fuck." I pull out my wallet, tossing some bills on the table.

"Where are you going?" Declan asks.

"To Ferndale."

Declan and Jonah shoot each other a look of surprise. "Right now?"

"Yeah, no time like the present to tell her I love her."

"This reminds me of that movie quote," Jonah says. *"When you realize you want to spend the rest of your life with somebody, you want the rest of your life to start as soon as possible."*

"When Harry Met Sally," Chelsea whispers in his ear.

I rush out of the bar. I have a few things to settle and take care of, but I'm ready to take a chance.

Chapter Twenty-six

Cat

I wake earlier than usual on Saturday morning and throw on yoga pants and thanks to Tristan, my new pink Cockadoodled*OOO* tshirt. The money from Booker's renovation has helped tremendously, but I still deliver breakfast here in Ferndale. For a little while longer anyways.

I pull the door open to *Pretty Pastries*, and smile to Susan. "Hey, I'm here for the deliveries."

"Let me get them for you." She heads to the back, and I glance around at the quaint shop and sigh, remembering the first time I saw Booker here.

I laugh to myself when I think about the donut he stole. There's a few chocolate glazed donuts sitting pretty on the silver tray behind the glass, but I don't bother getting one.

"Here you go," Susan says, handing me a single pink box. "There was only one this morning."

"Oh, ok, thanks."

Ten minutes later, I pull up to a row of cream-colored cottages with flower boxes beneath the windows and park my truck, grabbing the box from the side passenger seat.

With a hefty knock, I wait patiently, and when the door opens, I nearly drop the box of donuts.

"Hi, Cat."

"Booker, what are you doing here?" I want to pinch myself to wake me from this dream I've had so many times.

He leans against the door jam, folding his arms over his broad chest. And as always…he's completely nude.

I blush.

"Are those the chocolate glazed?"

I hold the box higher. "In the flesh." I've dreamt about his naked body so many times over the past few weeks. So. Many. Times.

"Come on in," he says, stepping aside so I can enter.

My mind whirls. Why is he here? In this house that's fully furnished? And why is he naked?

I spin around as he wraps a towel around himself.

"What are you doing here?" I ask again.

He steps closer. "I had to ask you a question."

"You came all the way here to ask a question?" I set the box of donuts down on the black coffee table and cross my arms. "Go on, then."

"If I moved from LA, rented a cute little cottage, and decided to live here, would you date me?"

He cocks a brow, waiting for my answer. A smile breaks free, and my heart beats faster. "Well, that depends…"

"On what?"

"Do you ever plan on breaking my heart?"

He wraps his arms around my waist, leaning in close to my lips. "Never," he whispers before kissing me.

The End

Epilogue

The sea calls to me. The Pacific wanting a word, but I can't focus on anything but her.

She's down by the shore, collecting rocks with her son.

It's a perfect backdrop for the kind of day I want to have for the rest of my life.

I step closer, not yet making my presence known as I continue watching the two of them together.

When I made the decision to lay it all on the line, I spoke with my mother about it first. She was more than thrilled to know I was happy.

I take another step, my heart pounding in my chest as I hold the rock I found on the beach six months ago in LA. The white rock.

Cooper sees me and takes off in a sprint toward me.

I pick him up and swing him into a hug. "Hey, little man," I say as I set him down.

I blink at Cat, her blue eyes are lit with questions and hopefully answers dwell there too.

"Want to see some of the rocks we picked out?" Cooper says, excitedly.

"Well, I found a rock just for you," I say, showing him the rock in my outstretched hand.

Catherine moves closer, not saying a word, just watching and listening to the exchange between me and her son.

Cooper takes the rock in his own tiny hand and smiles. "It's perfect."

I smile at his assessment. "I brought it for you."

"Where did you find it?" he asks, turning it over to inspect it.

"Los Angeles."

His eyes grow wide as he races over to his mom to show her.

"That's great," she says, quietly.

I step closer, drawing near to the main prize of my life.

"Did you bring mom a rock too?" Cooper asks.

Normally they scour the beach together, while I stay home to write. But, today is a different kind of day.

"I sure did. One nice hard rock." My eyes catch Cat's and a hint of playfulness passes between us.

"Let's see it," Cooper says.

"No, no." Cat puts her hands on Cooper's shoulder, obviously wanting to stop the inside joke before it goes any further.

But, it's not a joke. I do have a rock for her.

I stop, and my eyes meet Cat's as I lower to one knee. I pull out a black box from my pocket, and hold it out to her.

Her eyes fill with tears. "What are you doing?" she asks, her voice shaky.

"What I should have done a long time ago. Catherine Wells, I had given up on most things before I met you. I had ensured I'd never fall in love. I was so afraid to ever take a chance on anyone. So afraid of being let down like I had in my past." I take a deep breath as a teardrop slides down her cheek. "But, not anymore. Cat, I love you."

I open the box, and she smiles with tears shining in her eyes at the sight of the diamond ring gleaming up at her.

"Cat," I say. "I didn't have the best beginning in life. But, I want to have the perfect ending. Will you marry me? I promise I won't ever leave you. I promise I'll let you have every donut and every rock you set your eyes on. I want to be with you and Cooper always."

I smile to the woman I love, in the spot where I met her so many months ago, and stand.

"Say yes, Mommy," Cooper whispers, and Cat and I both share a look of joy.

I step closer, wrapping my arm around her waist. I press my forehead to hers. "I'll wait forever for your yes."

I lean in and kiss her. A soft, chaste kiss and smile as I pull back.

She flings both her arms around my neck, pulling me closer. "Lucky for you, you won't have to. Yes."

My whole world falls right into place. All the pieces of my fucked up existence mend together, and I'm happy.

THE END

Sneak Peek, Love Doctor

DECLAN

And Booker and Cat lived happily ever after. But just like any couple they have issues, but they're happy.

And having my best friend move way up North to Ferndale sucks ass. But, I'm too busy with school to worry about that. He's happy, so I'm happy for him.

Besides I'm too busy for anything.

I have the USMLE to take soon, and then it'll be official—I'll be a doctor.

Sure, it'll be hard.

Sure, I've been studying my whole life for this.

Sure, it'll take determination.

And I won't let anything get in my way.

Not even my sister's best friend, Gidget.

Even if she is probably the sexiest little thing I've ever seen.

LOVE DOCTOR releases early 2018.

Acknowledgements

Thank you for taking a chance on this book. I loved writing this story, and I hope you enjoyed it as well.

When I came up with the idea for this book, I knew I wanted Booker to have a job as kind of a flirt coach/mentor. Then the idea of being paid to be a jerk to someone came to life. Now, I know he doesn't have the most conventional job, and some may not like his job at all.
But, so is the land of fiction. With so many books out there, and plots, it's sometimes hard to find something original. Hopefully I was able to take a light, fun storyline and add some darkness and tragedy. As I like to do sometimes.
Oh, by the way this little section isn't edited. It's the day before Halloween and I'm on a ton of meds for an ear infection, so I'm just rambling some stuff about this story.
I love a story with a shocking twist.
Not all of my books have them, and not all future books will, but it's always a nice little surprise.
So, what's next for Logan Chance? Well, Dark Don is a little novella I started in my newsletter and FB group. It sort of took off, and now I'll be publishing it in December. So, be sure to sign up for my newsletter to know when that is all taking place.
Subscribe to my newsletter: http://eepurl.com/cSIuu1
I'll include a chapter in the end here.

After that Love Doctor, Declan's story will be released. I haven't a clue as to what his story is yet, but I'm sure there'll be a ton of sparks and magic.

I love hearing from my reader's, so if you'd like to connect with me, just follow these links.

www.loganchance.com
Facebook: www.facebook.com/loganchanceauthor
Twitter: www.twitter.com/loganchance85

The place I hang out most online is my FB group. I'm a huge Star Wars fan, and this group we come together, play games, do giveaways, talk about books, and so much more. I'd love for you to join.
https://www.facebook.com/groups/LoganChanceTDS/

The reason I picked Ferndale, California.

I urge you to Google this little Northern California town. As I was writing the story, well plotting it, I wanted a small town.

Having never been to California, I wasn't too sure if they even had the kind of town I was looking for. And was there a town like that near LA.

I came across the city of Ferndale, and fell in love. It's nestled right up against the Redwood Forest, and is home to only about 1400 residents.

And I also wanted a coastal city with whale watching. The Victorian-style homes are unlike any homes I've ever seen before. The town has a lot of character. With its historic village and artsy culture. I felt it was the perfect spot for Booker and Cat to raise Cooper.

A little bit about me. I'm Logan Chance from Boston, and moved to Florida. As anyone can tell you, I love to joke around and have fun. I'm a huge Star Wars and Superhero (well Marvel) fan. I love to get to know my readers, and I love writing hot stories you'll love.

If you haven't yet, check out my other books:

Like A Boss
Love A Boss (Boss Duet Book 2)
Sex Me Novella Series
All standalones
Date Me
Study Me
Save Me
And
Break Me

A new sexy romcom standalone Playboy
Meet Jonah and Chelsea
Synopsis:
They call me a playboy.

Sure, I like to have fun with the opposite sex, but hey, in my line of work, who wouldn't?
My name's Jonah and I work for Bunny Hunnies, a swimsuit magazine. Calling the shots, and taking pictures of gorgeous women is every man's fantasy, including mine.

That is, until Chelsea Sincock walks onto the set of one of my shoots.

I've known Chelsea since before she was this hot as hell vixen wearing nothing but a bikini.

What is she doing here?
Does her brother, Declan, know?
Did I mention he's my best friend?

This is going to be hard, I mean difficult, to work with her. And the more I gaze at her from behind the lens, the more I realize I'm in way over my head.

Amazon: http://amzn.to/2ihbrTf

Here's a little preview of Dark Don, releasing December
Chapter One
Rhiannon

It takes a lifetime to fall in love, and for me, a moment to fall out. Right now, on my knees, in front of my executioner, is when I fall out. I hate him. Red trickles from his knuckle, down his fingertip, forming a red teardrop that falls on the tip of his designer shoe. It splatters and spreads across the glossy black leather. Such a shame his five hundred dollar shoes are ruined.

My scalp screams for mercy when he fists my hair tighter and yanks my head back. His handsome face I dreamt about for years is contorted into a mask of rage I don't recognize.

"Answer me, Rhiannon," he demands.

"No." My knees scrape against the pavement when he pulls me closer.

He bends down, until his icy blue eyes are an eyelash width from mine. "Rhi," he whispers. "I won't show you any mercy."

"I don't want your mercy, Xavier," I whisper back. "Kill me." The lifeless eyes of my bodyguard lying an arms width away tell me that's probably not the wisest thing to say to the man who ended his life moments ago. I don't give a fuck, though.

I've loved this monster since he was ten years old. Now, I feel nothing. I'm glad he never knew how I felt about him. My nanny's son with the bright blue eyes who wrote poetry and kept me company when I was five is gone. In his place is a cold blooded killer. Like my father.

His warm lips brush against my ear. "What about Ian?"

My heart races. "You wouldn't."

His suited men watch in the darkened parking lot, waiting to see who comes out the victor in this battle of wills.

He pulls me to standing. "No? Haven't you learned yet I mean what I say?"

"Do it," I taunt. A muscle ticks in his jaw. "I don't want this life."

The breeze rustles through his dark locks. He releases my hair and turns away. "Put her in the car," he orders.

His henchmen get no resistance from me as they lead me to the black sedan.

I'll figure a way out of this. Just like when we were kids and played kidnap the princess. Except, this time, Xavier isn't smiling and laughing. And this time I'm not the princess of some imaginary land. I'm a different kind of a princess. Something I want no part of. A Mafia princess. And Xavier isn't my white knight coming to rescue me. He's the dark Don willing to kill me to get what he wants.
Power.

Dark Don is a dark mafia romance. It's very different from what I usually write, and like I was saying it was a little project my group and I did. They picked the genre and character names. Be on the lookout for it in December 2017

Love Doctor, Declan's story will be available beginning of 2018.

Please consider leaving a review to let me know what you thought of this story. And thank you for reading.

Thank you so much to the many supporters, bloggers, readers, and friends who have shared my work. I appreciate you more than you'll ever know.
Thank you.